THE DARK ONE

VICIOUS LOST BOYS BOOK TWO

NIKKI ST. CROWE

BLACKWELL HOUSE

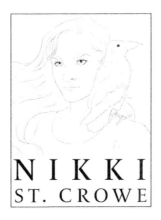

N I K K I
ST. CROWE

PUBLISHED BY BLACKWELL HOUSE LLC

ACKNOWLEDGMENTS

This book would not be possible without the help of several readers.

We can all agree that in the original *Peter and Wendy*, the depiction of Native characters was extremely problematic. When I set out to do a Peter Pan retelling, it was important to me to keep the Native presence on the island, but it was of the utmost importance that it be done in the right way.

I have to thank several sensitivity readers for helping me portray the twins and their family stories in *The Dark One* in a way that was accurate and respectful to the Native culture, even if the twins reside in a fantasy world.

So a huge THANK YOU to Cassandra Hinojosa, DeLane Chapman, Kylee Hoffman, and Holly Senn. You were extremely helpful and I appreciate your time, energy, and feedback!

Any mistakes or inaccuracies that remain in this book are entirely my own.

BEFORE YOU READ

The Vicious Lost Boys Series is a reimagining of *Peter and Wendy*, though all characters have been aged up and are 18 and over. This is not a children's book and the characters are not children.

Some of the content in this book may be triggering for some readers. If you'd like to learn more about CWs in Nikki's work, please visit her website here:

https://www.nikkistcrowe.com/content-warnings

To all the girls who have broken and mended.

"...there was a greedy look in his eyes now which ought to have alarmed her, but did not."

- J. M. Barrie, Peter and Wendy

1

PETER PAN

TWO SHADOWS LEAP FROM THE BOX IN MY HAND.

Two shadows.

It catches me so off guard that both of them slip through my grip.

One goes left, disappearing into the branches of the Never Tree, and the other goes right.

"Fucking hell. Get them!"

The one on my right knocks over several liquor bottles. They hit the floor with a resounding smash and liquor goes everywhere.

The leaves of the Never Tree rattle and the little pixie bugs blink with frenzied energy.

The twins go left. Vane and I go right.

I follow the shadow—*my shadow* because I would know it anywhere—out the open balcony doors. It disappears over the stone railing.

Hand to the railing, I leap over it too and hit the ground two stories down with a loud thud. The ground reverberates and the Lost Boys look up from the revelry just as the shadow leaps over the fire pit, embers sparking into the night.

Vane is beside me in an instant. "There," he says and points to the writhing shadows near the firecracker bushes.

I snap my fingers at the Lost Boys. "None of you fuckers move."

My skin is crawling and my stomach is twisted into knots. I've been waiting decades for this.

The Shadow of Life is mine by right. I have to claim it. I don't know what'll happen to me if I don't.

Vane and I stalk it, trying to cage it in.

The darkness quivers as we draw near. Behind us, the Lost Boys are silent as they watch and somewhere in the distance, the wolves howl.

The island knows the shadow has returned.

"If I miss it, you get ready to catch it," I tell Vane.

"I know how to handle a shadow," he says.

"Your black eye says otherwise."

He scowls at me.

We draw closer.

Closer still.

The hair lifts along the back of my neck and along my arms. I'm less than two feet away. This close to having what is rightfully mine.

Heart drumming in my head, I still my body, ready to leap at the exact right moment.

The shadow is mine. It will be mine. I just have to—

I lunge for it. The shadow dodges me and darts away.

"Fuck!" I yell and Vane and I give chase.

The forest parts for the damn thing, while leaves and branches pull at my hair, my shirt. We follow it to the lagoon, then down the length of the shore, then back into the forest along the path that leads to the road.

My chest tightens as we run. Sweat beads on my forehead and pours down my back.

I'm going to get it. I have to get it.

We burst from the path onto the dirt road and then two miles down and—

"Vane!" I shout. "We're running out of ground."

"I know!" he yells back. "I see it."

We pick up the pace. The shadow must sense us, because it flies through the night as if it were born of nothing but nightmares. And maybe it is. My own personal nightmare. Because nothing matters if I don't have it.

The window is fucking closing, what is left of my territory shrinking.

"Vane!"

He snatches at it. The shadow springs in the opposite direction, leaps off the trunk of a tree. I claw at the air, feeling the tug of it, the cool rightness of it.

But I'm too late.

So close and yet too far.

The shadow evades me and darts away.

And disappears into the darkness of Captain Hook's territory.

2

The leaves of the Never Tree shudder as the shadow darts around the branches. The pixie bugs wink out and go dark.

"You got eyes on it?" Bash asks.

"Over here," I answer.

The shadow is hunched at a split in the tree.

If I had my wings, I'd fly up to snatch it.

Everything is harder without wings. Sometimes the ache in my back, the space where they once were, aches like they are there, like I've just returned from a long afternoon flying among the clouds.

Bash comes around the tree trunk, his gaze trained on the canopy above us. "How do you want to do this?"

"Fuck if I know."

"Which shadow do you think it is?"

"My guess? The dark one. Pan will be pulled to his shadow, probably without even thinking about it."

Bash shifts to our fae language because no one but us can understand it.

If we catch it, he says and lets the thought trail off.

I know, I answer.

You think Pan will want one of us to have the death shadow? Hard to say what he wants. What do you want?

My twin gives me a pointed look.

If Bash or I were to claim the dark shadow, our little sister Tilly would hate us for having more power. But she made her decisions. And to see her face when one of us walks in as Neverland's Dark One....

I smile to myself as my twin's voice echoes in my head.

Let's nab it first. Then we can plot our revenge.

We close in.

"How about if one of us goes up?" I suggest. "Force it down."

"Rock-paper-scissor you for it. Whoever loses goes up."

We're still watching the branches as the leaves rattle again and the shadow shifts.

"Hurry up," I tell him.

"I'm ready. I'm waiting for you."

I snort and put my fist in the cup of my opposite hand.

"*Rock-Paper-Scissor-Shoot*," we say in unison and look away from the tree just long enough to see who has won.

"Rock? Really, Bash?" I say with a laugh. I went with paper. Bash always goes with the rock because he's predictable. "Looks like you're going up," I tell him.

"Yes, I know how the game works, asshole." He repositions himself beneath one of the lower hanging branches, then slowly wraps his hands around it, poised to leverage himself up. As children, we spent hours in the craggy, twisty trees of the fae forest. We'd climb up, then fly down, then climb up again.

"Be ready to catch it," Bash whispers.

I have my knees bent, hands out. "Of course, I'm ready. I'm always ready."

He hoists himself up. The branch dips with his weight. The shadow grows long in the tree.

"Slowly," I tell him and follow his movements.

"I know what I'm doing."

The shadow jitters and the branch shakes. Above us in the ceiling rafters, the parakeets are chirping loudly, sending out a shrill warning.

Bash gets his footing and crouches low on the branch to keep his balance as he inches forward, the bark scraping loudly beneath his boots. The shadow constricts, growls.

"Careful!"

"I am careful!" he hisses.

The shadow leaps to the next branch. Bash readjusts and I dart beneath the new branch.

If my twin or I possess the Death Shadow, everything will change. When our sister banished us from court, we lost almost everything we were.

To be powerful again...

Bash has the shadow backed against a V in the branches. The shadow vibrates. Is it afraid? Or maybe it's—

The shadow lunges. There's a deep, guttural roar from the thing and the pixie bugs fly out from the tree in a bright, neon swarm. The parakeets go eerily silent as Bash makes a wet, choked sound.

Then I smell the blood.

The shadow flies from the tree just as Bash tips over backwards.

"Bash!" I try to catch him but I'm not quick enough and he hits the floor on his back, a strangled breath rasping from his throat.

There is blood everywhere.

Fucking *everywhere*.

"Where are you hurt?" I say and scramble over him. His hand is clutched at his neck, blood gurgling between his fingers as he struggles for air.

"Darling!" I scream. "Winnie!"

She races into the room and stops when she sees the spreading veil of blood.

"Get a towel," I tell her. "Hurry!"

Bash's eyes are wide, blood staining his lips. He's trying to tell me something, but he can't get the words out.

"We are fae princes," I tell him. "Fae never die. Do you hear me?"

Tears are purged from the corners of his eyes as he gasps for air.

He is half of me.

If he dies, I will die with him.

If I am sure of nothing else, it's that.

3

WINNIE

GET A TOWEL.

Get a towel?

I don't know where anything is in the house.

I go to the kitchen because that seems a likely place and start opening cupboards. My heart is pounding against my ear drums and my hands are shaking.

There was so much blood.

Bash...*oh god*.

I feel sick.

How much blood can a fae prince lose? I don't know enough about Neverland or the magic that's here. I don't know anything about anything.

Yanking open the last cupboard, I let out a cry of relief when I find a stack of towels. I grab several and race back to the loft.

Kas has Bash upright, half in his lap. He's torn off his shirt, ripped it into shreds so he can wind the fabric around his brother's throat.

The blood on the hardwood floor is like a crude abstract painting, smeared and puddled and spreading fast.

That's too much blood.

And Bash is too damn pale.

"Hurry, Darling," Kas says, his voice wavering.

I race to his side, crash to the floor, slip in the blood, right myself. Together, we press the towels to Bash's throat.

Where is Pan? Vane? If Pan got his shadow, maybe there's something he can do. He's supposed to be all-powerful, right?

Bash's eyes are glassy and faraway.

"What do we do?" I ask.

"I don't know, Darling." Kas is on the edge of tears. "I don't fucking know."

He has his brother in his arms, cradling him against his chest.

"Can fae...I mean...don't you heal?"

"Yes, but blood loss..." He clenches his teeth and squeezes his eyes shut. "Too much is too much," he says when he looks at me again.

I swallow against the lump growing in my throat and take Bash's hand in mine. His fingers are cold and limp.

Before I came to Neverland, before I met the twins, I didn't even believe in fairies.

Hell, I nearly killed Bash when I said *I don't*—

Wait.

"Kas."

He glances at me, barely seeing me.

"Remember when you told me that if you say you don't believe in *you-know-what*, it kills you?"

He licks his lips. There's blood smeared across his face. "Yes, I remember." His voice wavers. I am seeing the hope slip from his eyes and it makes my chest ache and my stomach knot.

"That's such a simple thing, but a potent weapon. Right?"

"What are you getting at, Darling?"

"It must be magic?"

"I suppose."

"So what happens if you say the opposite? What happens if you say, 'I believe in fairies?'"

Bash jerks and makes a strangled moan.

Kas looks down at his brother, then back up at me, his eyes wide. "Do it again."

"I believe in fairies." I squeeze Bash's hand. "I believe in fairies."

Bash takes a gasping breath.

"Again, Darling."

"I believe in fairies!"

Bash rolls out of Kas's grip onto all fours and sucks in air.

"Holy shit," Kas says. "That fucking worked."

"Are you okay?" I ask Bash and have to fight the urge to reach out for him.

He rolls again and collapses on his back, blinking up at the beamed ceiling. "Fucking hell," he says. "That was—"

"*Fucking horrible*," Kas says.

"Terrifying," I add.

"A wild adventure," Bash finishes.

Kas smacks him. "Fucker. I thought you were fucking dead!"

He blinks again and touches the skin around his throat. "I thought I was too. But come on, brother. Dying would be an awfully big adventure."

"I hate you. You royal prick."

"I need a drink." Bash gets up.

These boys make my head spin. I'm still shaking, cold, and a little delirious with the terror of having watched the life nearly slip from Bash's eyes. He's still soaked in his own blood but has already moved past nearly dying.

"Where's Pan?" he asks.

"Haven't seen him yet," Kas answers, still sitting on the floor in a pool of his brother's blood. He still looks shaken and distant.

The blood squelches beneath Bash's boots as he makes his way to the bar.

I bring my hands up and find them smeared in crimson too.

I think I also need a drink.

"Here, Darling," Kas says and gets up, cleaning himself off with one of the extra towels. He offers me his hand, but it's still stained crimson with blood.

I take it and Kas lifts me easily to my feet.

As we cross the loft, Pan and Vane come up the winding staircase.

Immediately, the energy changes.

Pan looks at the blood on the floor, and the twins and I covered in it, and says nothing.

He makes his way to the liquor, grabs a random bottle and pulls out the stopper with a pop.

Something is wrong.

This doesn't seem like a man who is celebrating a victory.

He slings back the booze, his Adam's apple sinking low as he guzzles it down.

When he finally comes up for air, there is a barely constrained rage tightening in the muscles and tendons in his arms. A vein swells in his forehead.

"Did you find your shadow?" Bash dares to ask.

Vane gives a quick shake of his head. More warning than answer.

Pan sways on his feet.

The hair along the nape of my neck rises.

Pan curls his hand around the liquor bottle and lobs it at the wall. It shatters, rum spraying in the air, glass plinking against the floor. He grabs another and smashes that too. Then runs his arm down the length of the bar, destroying everything in his wake.

"Get her out of here," Vane says as he goes for Pan.

"Come, Darling." Kas captures me in the wide span of his bloody arms.

Pan roars. Smashes more liquor. Roars again. He grabs an end table and lobs it at the wall. The wood explodes like a bomb.

My gut turns.

"He didn't get it," I say, looking over Kas's shoulder as he steers me away. "He lost his shadow and the dark shadow is gone and Bash nearly died and—"

"It's going to be all right." Kas steers me into my room and shuts the door behind us.

"How can you say that? Your brother almost died. This was supposed to be it. Pan found his shadow. He was supposed to get it back and everything—"

"Winnie." Kas takes my face between his hands. We are covered in carnage. Beyond my room, Pan continues to smash and break and rage. "Listen to me, Darling. It's going to be all right."

"Is he always like this?"

"Does the Never King have a temper?" He snorts. "Yes. Very much so."

"He's terrifying."

"He'll cool down."

"He didn't get his shadow."

"It would seem so."

"It's all my fault."

"What? No." The fine lines around his eyes deepen as he frowns. "How can you say that?"

"My ancestors took it from him. He lost it—*twice*—because of the Darlings."

"No." Kas shakes his head. "My mother conspired to take it. The Darling was just a means to an end."

I peer up at him on the verge of tears. I hate fucking crying. Kas tucks my hair behind my ear with a soft caress of his fingertips.

It makes me shiver.

"Your mother was Tinker Bell, wasn't she?" I ask. He nods. "How can you be here, with Pan, when he killed her?"

He turns me toward the bathroom, his hands on my shoulders, steering me. "Our mother was a fucking bitch." He flicks on the light. "She was jealous of any woman who got near Pan. She wanted to be the queen to Pan's Never King. When Pan turned her down, she went to the next best and married our father, the fae king. She was just a common house fae who was greedy for so much more." He turns on the tap in the bathtub, testing the water. "She had one thing going for her—she was gorgeous and so ice cold, it burned. My father wanted to soften her. He never got his wish."

When the water is to his liking, he puts in the stopper and the tub starts to fill. He comes over to me and grabs the hem of my dress and coaxes me to lift my arms.

"Why did you kill him?" I ask.

He pulls the dress off in one fluid motion. "Because he was greedy for something too."

"What?"

"Power."

"Everyone on this island hungers for power."

"Yes, amongst other things." His gaze takes in the sight of me naked and covered in blood. I notice the bulge at his crotch and itch to take him in my hands. Is it fucked up if tragedy makes me want to disappear into pleasure? If blood and carnage make me want to touch so I can stop thinking and feeling?

Maybe it does. Maybe we're all a little fucked up and vile. Maybe that's why I feel like I might actually belong here.

My eyes roam over Kas's body, shirtless, in nothing but black pants. The straight lines that make up his tattoo undulate once they reach his abs. I reach out and trail one of the lines from his chest down his torso. His abs constrict even more beneath my touch and I'm suddenly pulsing with need.

"That was clever, what you did." His voice is quiet and edged in restraint. "You saved my brother's life. I will not forget that."

"It was just words."

"It was magic." He taps just above my breast, right over my heart. My nipples peak at his nearness and I can't help but arch my back, shifting closer to him. "Magic and a determination to keep him."

"I made a choice to come back here with you. With *all* of you."

I let my finger stay on the tattoo line as it passes his navel and disappears beneath the waistband of my pants.

But just as I'm prepared to hook into him, he snatches my wrist. "Get in the bath, Darling. Clean up." He drops my arm. "Don't come out until we tell you."

"You're leaving me?" I reach out for him, but he's already out of my range.

"If I stay in here much longer, Darling, I'll be bending you over the edge of the tub and fucking you until your ribs are bruised."

I straighten my shoulders. "Maybe I want that."

"I don't," he says. "When I finally get my cock in that tight pussy, it will not be out of desperation. Clean up and get some rest." He stops outside of the bathroom and looks at me over his shoulder. His dark hair is still wound up in a bun, but several strands have fallen out and hang stringy and bloody along his face. He is a sight. A bold, bloody, gorgeous sight. "Be a good girl," he tells me, "and do as I say."

Then he's gone.

Kas is the nicest of the group, which is exactly why when he commands me, it's almost hotter than when the others do.

It's like seeing the wolf pull back the sheep's clothing, baring razor-sharp teeth.

4

BASH

IT TAKES PAN AN HOUR TO CALM DOWN AND BY THEN, HE'S smashed most of the liquor. I get it, he's pissed he lost his shadow—*again*—but does he have to waste precious amounts of rum while expressing his vexation?

I think not.

At least he didn't have his throat slit by the dark shadow.

That thing was fucking brutal.

We might all be fucked if we cross paths with it. Perhaps it's best to let that one lie. I think I might understand Vane's piss-poor attitude a little more. Can't imagine letting that sort of darkness live in my veins.

A shiver makes my shoulders bunch up just thinking about it and I take a long swig of a bottle of rum I managed to save from Pan's brutal hand. The liquor helps drive some of the chill away. I feel like I had my soul torn out through my asshole. Everything hurts and my head is pounding. Is it safe for the Darling to come back out? I could use that sweet pussy wrapped around my dick.

Glass crunches beneath Vane's boots as he fetches one of the remaining bottles of bourbon and then hands it to Pan. Pan takes it, chest heaving, sweat coating his forehead.

The Never King does not like to lose.

"Drink," Vane orders. Pan drinks, strangling the neck of the bottle like he wants to wring the life from something else. I guess I don't blame him. He lost his shadow, the Death Shadow is loose, and now Hook might get his hands on power he does not deserve.

I take another swig of my own bottle and feel my brother watching me.

What? I ask him.

How are you feeling?

I'm fine. Healed by a Darling. I'd say I'm better than ever.

Kas frowns at me.

Vane scowls at us. "Quit that shit. You two got something to say, you say it out loud."

Kas's frown deepens. Pan drops into one of the leather chairs, the bottle propped on the rise of his knee, his head lolled back.

"Now what?" I ask. Let us be done with this so I can get my Darling.

Pan's eyes are closed. None of us speak.

The front door bangs open down below and a cacophony of sound rises up to the loft.

Some of the Lost Boys have returned from town with lost pussy in tow.

The girls' giggles are not unlike the tinkling of fairy bells.

Pan's eyes open.

Not that long ago, before Darling, we'd be down there

taking what we want. Now...now I'm not so sure just any wet cunt will do.

Whatever we might have done is decided for us because the girls come up of their own accord. They've been here before. They've bobbed on our dicks, had a mouthful of our cum.

"Hey," the girl at the front calls as she saunters over to the king. He watches her come over with hooded eyes.

I can't remember the girl's name, but she's the leader of this cohort. Libby or some shit like that.

She sits on Pan's lap. He lets her.

A few others come to the couch and fill in the space between my brother and me. We may not be kings, but we are princes, and even if we're banished, we still hold a certain undeniable currency.

I am tempted to touch.

I am reluctant to touch.

The fuck is this?

I am not a man who knows the shape of reluctance.

Libby hooks her arms around Pan's neck and leans into him. He takes another long drink of the bourbon. "Have you missed me?" she asks him and bats her eyelashes.

The one beside me crosses her legs, letting her skirt ride up her milky thighs. "How are you, Bash?"

This one I remember. Cora. I've fucked her a few times. Made her cry a few more. She's as much a whore for dick as she is a whore for attention. But I don't have the capacity to give her what she wants.

"You're such an arrogant prick," she told me last time she was here.

"Cora, dear," I'd said, "as if I care what you think."

Of course, at the time, I was buried balls deep in another girl.

Thinking this, my cock twitches and I have to fight the urge to grab her and haul her onto my lap.

What stops me?

The awareness of Darling just down the hall.

I care what she thinks and I don't know how I feel about that.

"Why are you giving me that look?" Pan says to Vane.

Vane is the only one without a girl by his side. Given the chance, they'd all let him chase them, but they know better than to try. Vane is as interested in them as he is in the art of folding cocktail napkins.

"What do you think your little Darling will do if she walks in here right now and sees you with *that* on your lap?" Vane says.

Libby's mouth drops open. "Hey!"

Vane cuts his gaze to the girl and she quickly clamps her mouth shut.

Pan sits forward and looks at the Dark One around the heaving swell of Libby's tits. "I am a king," he says, a little drunk. "I do what I want."

"You keep telling yourself that."

"We don't do *exclusive*." Pan says the latter like its edged in ick.

"Are you trying to convince me?" Vane counters.

"What the fuck is she going to do about it?" Pan says.

Vane leans back in his chair and opens his book. He's always got a book within reach. "She'll checkmate your ass before you even know you're sitting at the board."

Kas says to me, *When do you think Vane will admit he doesn't hate the Darling?*

I snort. *And ruin his reputation? Never.*

He's right, though, Kas says, *if Darling comes out here, she's going to be pissed.*

Pan's too drunk and angry to be thinking straight. I will enjoy the show when she does.

A dark-haired girl, one I don't recognize, slips closer to my twin. "My name's—"

"I don't care what your name is," Kas answers, barely giving her a look.

Who's the asshole tonight? I say.

Fuck off.

The Darling has you wrapped around her finger.

Kas gives me a heavy look. *She's got a finger for one and all.*

I laugh out loud. The girls frown at us, annoyed at being excluded from the conversation.

Vane settles into his book and Pan carries on with Libby like he's just daring Vane to say something. But he hasn't undressed her. He hasn't put his mouth on her. He hasn't fucked her.

I can see the truth in his actions.

Peter Pan is just as reluctant as I am.

5

AFTER MY BATH, I WRAP A THROW BLANKET AROUND MY SHOULDERS and curl into the wingback by the open windows and listen to the ocean down below. The room is dark save for the slant of moonlight. The air is cool on my bare legs as I prop my feet on the window sill.

I must fall asleep at some point, because I wake with a jolt later, and the ocean has quieted to a soft lapping against the pebbled beach.

Beyond the room, I hear girls laughing and a dark thing curls in my belly.

I toss the blanket aside and go to the closed bedroom door and set my ear to the cool wood.

There are definitely girls out there. I hear the distinct rumble of Kas and Bash talking.

Did they really banish me to my room and then decide to throw a party in my absence?

The rage that burbles up my throat is raw and sharp.

What was it Peter Pan said the other night? No one was

allowed to touch me. He thinks he's claimed me like some kind of possession? That he can do what he pleases with me with no consequences for himself?

Of course the Never King thinks the rules don't apply to him.

Kas told me to stay in my room until they told me to come out, but I'm not a fucking prisoner here. Not anymore.

I yank the door open and follow the slide of golden light from the hallway to the loft.

Smoke curls in the air. Pixie bugs glitter in the branches of the Never Tree amongst the sleeping, warbling parakeets.

And dotted around the room, and on the lap of Peter Pan, are a handful of pretty girls.

If I had to guess, they're mostly my age, though being that they're on the island, it's hard to say if they're mortal age or immortal. I still don't know how that all works. Who ages and who doesn't. Maybe no one does here. Maybe they're all trapped in time like a bug in a drop of ancient sap.

The room goes quiet when I come to a stop on the other side of the sectional couch.

The twins look up at me. There are several girls between them on the couch, but no one is touching. Vane is in one of the leather chairs, a book open between his hands. He barely gives me notice. A cigarette dangles from between his lips.

Peter Pan is in the chair beside Vane, a blonde girl on his lap. The girl regards me like I'm a piece of trash the ocean vomited to its shores.

Pan and I lock eyes.

His face tightens as we take the measure of one another.

I narrow my gaze at him, trying to slow my breathing and the elevated thump of my heart.

He doesn't have his shadow yet. He's not all powerful. Which means if I want to make a stand, now is the time, and there is a sudden, urgent need to get back at him for making my stomach knot up like it is, for making me feel like a territorial bitch even though I have no claim to any of them.

And maybe he's doing it on purpose. Maybe he wants to see what I'll do.

There is a barely perceptible uptick in his expression, a slight curl to his mouth as he senses the shift in my demeanor.

It's now or never.

I dart for the stairs.

Pan tosses the girl from his lap, and she protests in a high-pitched yelp before she hits the floor with a thud.

I feel him at my back giving chase, and goosebumps rise along my arms.

He's bigger than me, longer-legged and definitely faster. But I've spent enough time in old houses to know how to use them as I need.

When I reach the staircase, I tuck my dress under my ass and sit on the railing, then slide down its length.

When Pan tries to snatch me, he misses me by an inch and I leap to the ground floor a second later.

He takes several steps down before abandoning that idea and puts his hand to the railing, hoisting himself over it.

I'm already running. Already designing my revenge.

There's a fire crackling in the bonfire pit and over a dozen Lost Boys gathered around it. I pick the first one I see, leap into his arms, wrap my legs around his waist and mash my lips against his.

This isn't about pleasure.

It's about making a point. Unfortunately for the Lost Boy.

He goes rigid beneath me.

It doesn't take Pan long to catch up and wrench me away.

The Lost Boy blinks up at us, wide-eyed, his face devoid of blood. "Sorry, Never King. I didn't want to touch her. She just came at me!"

Pan rights me. "The fuck are you doing?"

"The fuck are you doing?"

"They're not allowed to touch you," he says and points vaguely at the Lost Boys. "They know that. You know that."

I cross my arms over my chest and cock out a hip. "They're not allowed to touch me," I say, "but you never mentioned *me* touching *them*. Based on that rule, I can touch all I want and I plan to. If you get to touch, I get to touch."

From the balcony, Kas and Bash snort their laughter.

Pan fumes. "Let's discuss this upstairs."

"No."

"No?"

The only sound is the crackling of the fire, the shudder of the palm fronds in the slight ocean breeze.

"*No*?" he repeats.

The Lost Boy I mauled takes a step back. The others haven't moved an inch.

Pan regards me like a naughty child. And then he's suddenly hoisting me over his shoulder in a fit of déjà vu.

"I'm not your property!" I yell and pummel his backside.

Of course, it's no use. Peter Pan is nothing but lean muscle and rock-solid hubris. He carts me up the stairs, barely noticing my fists against his muscular back.

When we pass the twins on the balcony, I push up. "Help me?"

"Sorry, Darling," Bash says with a devilish grin. "You got yourself into this one."

I deflate and hang limp as Pan carries me into the house. When we come into the loft, he snaps his fingers loudly and says, "Get the fuck out of here."

The girls scurry away, heels clomping down the main staircase.

Pan drops me into one of the leather chairs and points at me, silver rings glinting beneath the golden glow of the room. "I'm in no fucking mood."

"Funny, I wasn't in the mood to come out of my room and find some Neverland whore on your lap."

When he sits in the chair next to me, he scowls and spreads out his long legs. He puts a cigarette between his lips and opens a lighter with a snap of his fingers.

Once the flame is to the end, the paper and tobacco ignite and Pan takes a long pull.

The lighter snaps shut.

Smoke curls like the bands in an agate.

After he's exhaled, he props his elbow on the arm of the chair, the cigarette captured between his first two knuckles. He looks at me, blue eyes glittering in the light.

I'm hot and cold at once.

I wanted his attention and now I have it.

"I am a straightforward man," he says. "I don't like to play games. If you have something to say to me, Darling, say it to my face."

I breathe out through my nose.

What do I want to say? And how the hell do I say it? I'll admit, I didn't really have a plan beyond making him regret touching another girl.

But I guess that's the heart of it, isn't it? So best just to say it.

"I don't want to share."

He narrows his eyes.

"If I'm not allowed to touch anyone else, then neither are you."

Pan runs his tongue along the inside of his bottom lip. His eyes never leave my face and the weight of his gaze has me rubbing my thighs together to stave off some of the buzzing between my legs.

"We are four very hungry men. Do you really think you're capable of keeping up with our appetites?"

I don't even have to think about it. "Yes."

His gaze turns dark and dangerous and I think maybe he knew where this was leading all along. He drew the map and I followed the X right into his trap.

"Then show me," he says.

"How?"

"You want all four of us, then get on your knees and put that mouth to work. Show me you can be our little Darling whore."

The buzzing intensifies and my clit swells to a needy bud.

Well, fine then. He wants a performance, he's going to get one.

I stand. He takes another long drag from the cigarette, letting the smoke leak out past his lips in a dense cloud before sucking it back in.

I'm tight and taut and more excited than I should be.

I move to sink to the floor in front of him but he shakes

his head just once. "Twins first. I want to watch you choke on them."

The hard edge of his words is meant to frighten me off, but if that's his plan, he doesn't know me very well. Because my stomach is full of wings and my pussy is throbbing.

I suspect if the Never King orders the fae princes to fuck my mouth till I cry, they will.

I suspect if they do, I'll like it.

When I turn for the twins, Bash already has his cock in hand as if he's been waiting for this all night.

I cross the room and sink between his legs, the rough-spun rug biting into my knees. Bash fists himself, stroking long and slow. Pre-cum already glistens on the head of his dick and he rubs it off with the pad of his thumb, then wipes it across my bottom lip.

There is an answering thrill in my pussy as I swipe my tongue over the sweetness.

"I've had that naughty little cunt twice," he says. "I will enjoy having your mouth too."

"Then what are you waiting for?" I challenge.

He groans deep in his chest, then takes a fistful of my hair and shoves me down around him.

The size of him in my mouth takes me by surprise and the air gets stuck in my throat as I try to adjust.

Bash rocks his hips forward as he drives me down on him, the head of his shaft hitting the back of my throat. I gag. He pulls out and I suck in a deep breath.

Pan says behind me, "Don't go easy on her, Bash. She wanted it, make her take it."

"Who am I to deny what the king demands?" Bash nudges me back, then rises to his feet. He slaps me in the face with his cock and I gasp in surprise.

"Don't stop, Darling. Go on." He's smiling at me, amber eyes bright.

I reposition and wrap my lips around him, bobbing up and down on him. He buries his hand in my hair and yanks hard on it as he guides me deeper.

"That's a good girl," he says. "Look at me."

I crane my head so I can meet his gaze and the dark satisfaction glittering in his eyes makes my belly soar and my clit throb.

I wish he was touching me. I wish his brother was fucking me. I wish...I wish...

"Just like that, Darling."

He pumps his hips, driving into me.

"Fuck, yeah."

I can't catch my breath and tears spring in my eyes as he hits the back of my throat. I breathe out quickly through my nose, trying to accommodate him, trying not to choke.

"Fuck, Darling."

The whole time, I can feel Pan's gaze on me, drinking me in.

There is something deeply exciting about being a show.

Bash pumps faster, fucking my mouth in a way that's more punishing than anything.

And when he finally spills inside of me, cum blooming on my tongue, I breathe in deeply, trying not to break until he's emptied himself. I'm shaking and hot and flustered and horny as hell.

Bash angles me up as he pulls out of my mouth. "Did you swallow it? Let me see, Darling."

I stick out the flat of my tongue.

Of course I swallowed it. I'm no slouch.

"Good girl," he says and then bends down to kiss me, long and deep, his tongue sliding over mine. When he pulls back, he rests his forehead against mine and says, "I fucking needed that more than you'll ever know."

"Maybe I needed it more than you did."

He chuckles to himself. "You're about to get more than you need. Kas," he says and straightens. "Get me some rope."

There is the thud of Kas's footsteps as he disappears and when he returns, there's a length of rope in his hands. It takes Bash less than two seconds to have my arms behind my back and tied at the wrists.

Bash stays at my back and keeps the tail of the rope in one hand while his other wraps around my throat. "Your turn, brother," he says.

Kas is already hard, but he hesitates, taking me in, bound and positioned for him.

My stomach is full of butterflies and my lips are wet and swollen. I can still taste Bash's cum on the tip of my tongue, but if this were a feast, I've only just had a taste.

Bash yanks the rope up, arching my body, forcing my chest out. I'm still wearing my dress, but it has a low collar and when Kas comes over to me, he runs his finger along the stitching and goosebumps bloom from my chest, beading my nipples.

He eyes the taut nubs through the material.

"Do you like to be used, Darling?" he asks, as if the answer matters.

Does it? No one has ever cared what I wanted.

"That's a complicated question," I say.

"Give me your best answer."

"Yes."

"Why?"

I close my eyes as his hand drifts lower, his clever

fingers teasing at my nipple through the material. I hiss out as an answering thrill dips to my pussy.

"Because it makes me feel good."

"And?"

He moves to my other breast, pinches my nipple hard, and new wetness seeps into my panties.

"And it makes me feel less alone."

Tears burn in my eyes, catching me off guard.

That was more than I wanted to admit. More truth than I'm comfortable with.

I don't want to be alone anymore.

Kas undoes his belt and the zipper bites loudly as it opens up tooth by tooth.

His cock strains against the dark material of his underwear. If I had use of my hands, I'd be helping him in earnest.

I've only had Kas once and that was after Pan had me over the table, while his twin fucked me from behind.

There was no time to pay attention.

Kas is bigger than Bash. Bigger than Pan too, I'd guess. Hard to say how he measures up against Vane.

I don't know if I can take all of Kas in my mouth.

Bash repositions his hand around my throat and angles me just right like I'm the stage and he the director, Kas our golden performer.

My heart is hammering in my eardrums.

My stomach is in knots.

I can do this. I can take the sheer size of him. I *will* take him.

He rubs the head of his dick over my lips and I dart out my tongue to meet him, causing him to groan deep in his chest. The feral sound of it sends a thrill down to my pussy.

He wants to linger, but I can already tell there's no time for that.

Dragging his thumb over my bottom lip, he dips into my mouth, making me suck him. "I might be fooling myself," he says, his eyes hooded, his voice hoarse. "Perhaps with you, Darling, there is only desperation."

And then he drives his dick into my mouth.

6

WINNIE

KAS FUCKS MY MOUTH FAST AND HARD UNTIL TEARS STREAM DOWN my face.

I do choke on him.

With my arms tied behind my back, I have no control over his pace and he is relentless.

He is desperate.

And he is far too big for my mouth.

When he finally comes, it shoots straight down my throat and when he pulls out, I gasp for air.

He staggers away and drops onto the couch, head lolled back at the ceiling where the pixie bugs are darting back and forth in an excited frenzy.

I know how they feel.

I pant out several more breaths as Bash comes around and wipes the tears from my face. "Such a good girl, aren't you, Darling?"

"Untie me," I say. "So I can take care of the king."

He smiles at me. "As you wish."

When the ropes are gone, I rub at my wrists to bring some of the feeling back to my hands.

I look over at Pan.

He's stretched out in the chair, his gaze distant. He's wearing dark denim and a dark t-shirt that skims the rise and valley of his biceps like a second skin.

Dark ink swirls down his arms, and several tendrils peek out around the collar.

He is an unholy sight.

And I will never stop sinning for him.

I move to stand to go to him but he tsk-tsks at me and shakes his head.

"Did I tell you to get off your knees?" he says. "You'll *crawl to me*."

The butterflies turn into a storm of desire and shame in my gut.

He wants me to *crawl* to him?

He thinks he's proving a point, that I can't stay in the game even though he swears he hates to play.

Everything is a game. Especially this.

Everyone is silent, waiting, wondering what I'll do.

I will not lose.

I am determined to be a feast for Peter Pan, make him a glutton for the taste of me.

I put my hands to the rug and crawl to him.

The book snaps shut in Vane's hands and my center of gravity sways at the mere thought of him watching me, my back bent like a serpent, my ass in the air.

Maybe if I put on enough of a show, he'll want in too.

I want to take and take from these men, hoard my spoils like a greedy queen.

When I reach Pan, he opens his legs for me so I can crawl up between them. His gaze is bright and satisfied as I unlatch his belt buckle and pull the leather through the clasp. The metal clanks. Pan watches.

He's straining against his pants as I undo the button and seeing the bulge of him lights a fire in my chest.

When I have the zipper open, I yank his clothes down, letting his cock spring free.

Rising up, I position my mouth over the swollen head of his cock and his body tenses up, waiting.

I take him in my hand, stroke him slowly, memorizing every ridge, every engorged vein.

He gnashes his teeth.

"I don't want to share," I tell him.

His nostrils flare.

"I don't want to find you with some girl from town sitting in your lap when I'm just down the hall. When it can be *me* in your lap."

I sit forward and put my lips an inch away from him and blow out a teasing breath. The head of his cock throbs at the anticipation of my mouth wrapping around him.

"Say it, Never King."

"Put that pretty little mouth on my cock and maybe I will."

I inch forward, drag the tip of my tongue over the glistening slit of his dick.

"Say it."

He groans and rocks his hips forward trying to meet me, so I sink to the base of his shaft and lick up the thick underside.

A puff of air escapes him.

I think he and I both know he could drive into me at any point, but the game is the game. And I intend to win.

The Never King is mine. And I'm going to make him admit it.

I go through the motions like I'm going to lick him again from base to tip, but I keep my mouth just a ghost against him, almost touching, not quite connecting.

The groan that rumbles in his chest is practically animalistic.

"Darling," he says.

"Yes?"

His eyes slip closed and he summons a deep, settling breath. "The only pussy I will have is your pussy." His eyes pop open again and he sits forward, grabbing me beneath the arms and whirling me around so that I'm the one in the chair and he's the one on his knees. "The only mouth that will come near my cock is your mouth." He bunches my dress up around my waist. "The only girl who will sit on my lap like a pretty little trophy is you." He hooks a finger in my panties and yanks them aside, baring me. "The only girl I will treat like my personal whore is you." He sits forward, putting his mouth just over my wetness, giving me a taste of my own medicine.

I tremble with anticipation.

"Will that suffice, Darling?" he says.

I nod emphatically. "Yes."

He flicks his tongue over my clit, but it's just barely a glance, a tease more than anything, but I still have the urge to crawl out of my skin.

"Say it again," he orders.

"Yes, that will suffice."

He slides his fingers up the seam of my panties, purposefully dragging the backside of his knuckles over my pussy, then my clit.

I shake with the pleasure of it.

"Yes, what?"

I sink into the plush leather chair. "Yes...Pan?"

He spits on my pussy, and slides two fingers up to meet my swollen nub. "Try again."

"*Yes*..." I inhale sharply when he slides back down and sticks his fingers deep inside of me. "Yes, my king."

"Good girl," he says and finally gives me what I want and need—his mouth on my pussy.

He licks and teases and fucks me with his tongue.

I writhe in the chair, but he has me caged.

I pant and moan at the ceiling.

He is relentless with his mouth.

The pleasure builds in my clit and when he adds a finger, fucking me with three, a high-pitched keening escapes my throat.

I can feel them all watching me.

And I don't care.

Somehow Pan has shifted the show, made me the audience and the performer.

I buck beneath him. He holds me tighter, his tongue sliding up my wet slit.

"Come for me, Darling," he says from between my thighs. "Come in my mouth."

I'm breathing too quickly and my head is swimming and my body is bright with need and desire. The wave rushes in as Pan flicks his tongue against my clit and his fingers fill me up.

I come so loudly, the sleeping parakeets wake and take flight in a flap of wings.

I thread my hand through Pan's hair and guide him over me as the orgasm pounds through me like an earthquake, shaking every bone.

There is nothing but the pleasure and the heat of it.

When I crash down on the other side, I'm slumped low

in the chair with Peter Pan still between my legs, his mouth soaked with my juices.

He slowly rises over top of me and the line of his shoulders blocks out the light so that all I can see is him.

"You want us, Darling, you have us, but you follow *my* rules. Do you understand?"

I take in several slow, measured breaths.

"Say it, Darling."

"Yes. Fine. I'll follow your rules."

"If you're hungry for cock, you have four to choose from. Four and no more." He hooks his hands around my thighs and yanks my ass to the edge of the chair. "If I catch you touching anyone else, I will not be happy." With my panties still askew, he nestles into my opening. "Tell me you understand."

"I understand."

He fills me up and I exhale quickly. His thrusting tempo shifts. Faster. Harder. He bends my legs up and pounds into me and I'm so wet and he's so hard, we make a loud squelching sound as we fuck.

Pan drives into me, sinking me into the chair. He fucks me like he owns me and maybe in some ways he does.

Maybe I am his property.

Maybe I don't hate that idea.

Pan is relentless and my pussy takes the pounding.

I will take and take because there will always be power in it.

And I want to be powerful among these powerful men.

When Pan finally comes inside of me, I'm used up and sore and bright with satisfaction.

But there is one more.

One more cock to satisfy.

If he'll let me.

Pan pulls back and tucks himself away, then drops into the chair beside me.

I sit up and find Vane's mismatched eyes squarely on me.

He gives me a barely perceptible shake of his head.

But I'm not easily cowed.

I get up, cross the room, Peter Pan's cum dripping down my thighs.

Vane's chest rises with a deep breath.

My heart gets lodged in my throat.

In front of Vane, I sink to my knees yet again, but this time my hands are shaking and my mouth is bone dry with anticipation.

I reach forward to undo the button on his pants and Vane snatches me by the wrist as his violet eye goes black.

The terror slithers up my spine and sweat breaks out along my hairline.

Gulping down air, I try to quell the fear erupting into goosebumps on my skin.

I can do this. I can endure him and his terror and prove to him I'm strong.

I reach up with my other hand, determined to have him.

But before I know what's happening, I'm flown across the room and thrown up against a wall, Vane's hand wrapped around my throat.

7

WINNIE

THE SHOCK HAS THE AIR RUSHING OUT OF ME IN A USELESS GASP and Vane's hold on me tightens, closing off my air supply as he lifts me off my feet and I pedal uselessly for purchase.

The darkness of the Death Shadow surges around his eyes as his hair turns bright white.

"Vane! For Christ's sake!" Pan and the twins rush up behind us.

I can feel my face turning bright red as I struggle for oxygen.

"Let her go," Pan says.

The terror kicks up again in the base of my belly and crawls like a centipede up the center of me. My heart beats loudly in my ears.

"The Darling wants what she wants." Vane's voice has shifted along with his gaze. The Death Shadow turns him more demon than man so that his voice rumbles and echoes around us.

Tears spill over my lids and trail down my cheek.

I was not prepared for this.

I had no idea what I was getting myself into.

"Shhhh," he coos. "Save your tears for when it really hurts."

My eyes bulge from their sockets.

"Please let her go," Pan says, as the twins edge around us.

"She thinks she wants it," Vane goes on. "Let me prove to her why she shouldn't."

If I had air in my lungs, I'd be screaming.

I wrap my hand around Vane's wrist, the other scrabbles at his grip on me. I need air. I need air. Some kind of reprieve.

Fuck.

Maybe I am a stupid girl who knows nothing at all.

"Vane," Pan says again, just as the twins lunge.

I drop to the floor when Vane lets me go. On all fours, I gasp for air.

The twins grab each of Vane's arms and haul him back. Vane fights them and throttles Bash by the throat and tosses him aside like he is nothing at all. Kas comes next and gets a boot square in the chest. He flies through the air and slams into the trunk of the Never Tree and the branches shudder from the impact.

Vane turns on Pan next.

Pan holds up his hands. "Get your shit together," he says.

Vane stalks toward him.

"For fuck's sake, Vane."

I suck in oxygen and then put my back to the wall and use it to slide up to my feet.

When I try to speak, my voice comes out raspy and hollow. "Vane," I try.

"She's ours, isn't she?" Vane says, his voice still terrifyingly dark.

"You need to figure out how to control the shadow," Pan says, still backpedaling. "Or we're all going to end up dead."

"I am the shadow." Vane closes the distance between him and Pan. "I don't need to control it."

"Yes, you fucking do or I'll send you back to your island."

Vane lunges. Pan ducks. Vane swings again and catches Pan across the jaw. He staggers back and Vane takes the opening, catching Pan by the arm.

Darkness blooms from Vane's touch, spreading over Pan's tattoos, soaking into his skin deeper than ink.

What is that?

The darkness spreads up and up and eats away at the pale skin of Pan's throat.

"What's happening?" I croak. "Kas? What is happening?"

Kas shakes his head, wide-eyed. "He's going to kill him if he doesn't stop."

The inky tendrils stretch up the curve of Pan's jaw, turning his lips black.

"What do we do?"

Bash frowns. "I don't fucking know. No one can stand against Vane, other than Pan."

Pan grits his teeth as the darkness consumes him inch by inch. "Vane...for fuck's sake." Pan gasps out but Vane shows no signs of letting up.

"We have to do something," I say.

Peter Pan can't die.

"Vane!" I yell.

He turns just slightly, the line of his jaw meeting the rise of his shoulder.

"You can have me any way you need me."

"*Darling*," Kas says on a hiss. "The fuck are you doing?"

I edge closer, keeping my arms out to prove I mean him no harm.

Vane drops Pan and the darkness immediately recedes and Pan hunches over, hand clutched at his chest.

The Death Shadow turns to me and the terror edges back in.

He takes slow, deliberate footsteps stalking me like a predator stalking prey.

I back into the wall and step on a shard of glass with my bare foot and hiss at the bite of pain.

That's the least of my worries. I can look at the wound later.

But Vane's gaze wanders to the floor, to the footprint I've left in blood.

The pain is sharp and intense but it's nothing I haven't endured before.

As the blood spreads and the pain throbs through my nerves, I notice something else.

The terror has seeped away with the blood.

Vane frowns at me and the white disappears from his hair.

I breathe through the dull ache in my foot.

Vane's eyes return to their normal mismatched black and violet, but the anger is still cut into the line of his jaw.

The energy of the room has shifted. It is the quiet after the storm when the ocean has stopped churning and the sky has stopped crackling.

Vane rocks his shoulders back and takes in a long, deep breath and says, "Don't ever do that again," and then makes his way down the stairs and right out of the house.

8

PETER PAN

I hurry to Darling's side and brace her against my shoulder and nudge her calf. "Lift up," I order her and she does as commanded.

There's a nasty cut on the arch of her foot.

"Kas," I say.

"I'm on it." He disappears down the hall.

Bash opens one of the cupboards behind the bar and comes back with a towel and hands it to me.

"Hold on to me, Darling," I tell her, and she winds her arm around my neck as I lift her easily. I carry her to the couch and set her down in the corner so I can position her bleeding foot on my lap. Wet crimson is already seeping into my pants.

Kas returns with a first aid kit, and a needle and thread.

"It's not that bad!" Darling protests and tries to yank her foot back.

I hold her fast. "Do not fight me," I tell her. "It's a gaping wound. It'll heal faster if we suture it."

She falls back against the cushion. "Blades I can take. Needles...not so much."

I look over at her and find the edge of terror in her pretty green eyes. She is stronger than we want to believe, I think, but we all must dread something.

Not that long ago, the thing I feared most was losing the island.

With Darling's scent still on me and her blood soaking my clothing, that fear is changing shape right before my fucking eyes.

Seeing her bleeding, seeing the bruises starting to bloom around her throat from where Vane had her against the wall...

My gut twists and I don't want to let her go.

I don't want her to disappear like my shadow and slip off into the night and leave me alone, a hollowed man left with nothing but writhing darkness and a festering wound where my heart once was.

I am cold inside. I want to be warm.

I snap my fingers at the bottle of bourbon on the table and Kas fetches it for me so I can soak the rag. When I put it to Darling's foot, she hisses in return and flails in my grip.

"Hold still."

"It hurts."

"You were going to let Vane do with you what he pleased and you're complaining about a little bit of alcohol?"

She groans, knowing I'm right.

"We need to address the problem that is the Dark One," Bash says as he runs the needle through the flame from a lighter.

"One problem at a time."

Our new mantra, it would seem.

Once the blood is cleaned up, I can get a better look at the cut. It's about three inches long and still seeping. In Darling's world, they have anesthesia for this sort of thing. Here we have fae princes.

"Give her something for the pain," I tell them as Bash hands over the threaded needle.

"Lie back, Darling," Kas orders.

She gives us all a skeptical look.

"You'll let us fuck you into oblivion but not care for you when you're injured?" I say. I don't like that she looks like a wounded forest creature, trembling and clammy. "Please, Darling," I add. "Let me take care of you."

Wetness springs to her eyes and I think she's never had a gentle hand in her life. I can be brutal and fuck her and treat her like my whore, but I will care for her when she's wounded and she will submit to it, and I will prove to her that she can have both from me.

I will not betray her when she needs me the most.

Finally, she repositions and settles back against the cushions. I give Kas a nod.

Within seconds, Darling sighs out in relief. I don't have to see it to know that he's given her an illusion. Fae magic can be just as much about feeling as it is about sight.

"Good?" I ask Kas.

He nods. "She should be good for a while."

I set the needle to her flesh and start closing the wound. She barely notices.

"He nearly killed you," Bash says as he sits on the edge of the low table in front of me and watches me work.

"Yes, but he didn't."

"Only because Darling distracted him."

I have the wound half closed and growing smaller by the second. When you're constantly under threat from pirates, you quickly become an expert at tending to wounds. "He just needs to find a balance," I say, but even I know that's bullshit. Vane has been on Neverland for years. He's had the Death Shadow even longer. If he was going to find a balance, he would have by now.

"If you get your shadow back," Kas starts, "you think you can control him?"

"Hard to say."

Doubtful. Maybe.

Maybe I am a fool to even entertain the idea.

Once the wound is closed, I knot off the string and hand the needle to Kas. Bash is waiting with gauze and tape and the tin of fairy salve he makes regularly. With the lid already open, I scoop a finger in. The salve smells like Neverland earth.

I gently rub it into the wound before wrapping the gauze around it and taping it off.

"Keep the illusion going for a while," I tell them. "Let her rest."

Wherever she is, she's far gone from us and the loft.

Which is just as well.

My cock thickens as my mind conjures images of the twins fucking her mouth.

God, I love watching her get used.

But only by those I trust most. I wouldn't let those other fuckers get close enough to breathe the same air as her.

Vane was right about one thing—she knew how to play me.

The thought of anyone else laying a hand on her makes me want to break bones.

I look over at her splayed out on the couch, her legs still draped over my lap. Her skin is warm and soft beneath my hands. I wish I could curl into her side. I wish I could hold her to me.

The urge for both is foreign and ill-fitting.

I'm not usually territorial. I don't usually care enough to bother. But every inch of her pale skin is territory I want to conquer and make mine.

I need to get the fuck out of here before I fuck her again, before I use her more than I should.

Gently, I slide out from beneath her legs and then pull one of the throw blankets from the back of the couch and drape it over her tiny body. She curls into the warmth and moans when I push aside an errant lock of hair.

My gut clenches again but for a very different reason.

"I'll be back," I tell the twins. "Watch over her. Please."

"Of course," Kas says.

"She's as much ours as she is yours," Bash answers. "You don't have to tell us to watch over her."

The fae princes are pushing more than they used to.

One problem at a time.

I give them a quick nod before I go off in search of the Dark One.

I find Vane walking along the shore of the lagoon toward Marooner's Rock.

The spirits of the turquoise water crest the surface, hands and faces and flapping tails. They're trying to get closer to him. His shadow may not be from Neverland, but magic likes magic, regardless of its origins.

"Don't start with me," he calls even though I'm behind him and have not made a sound.

"I haven't said anything."

"I can hear you thinking."

"No, you can't."

"Then I can feel you thinking."

Smoke curls over his shoulder as he takes a hit from a cigarette.

I pick up the pace so I can catch up to him. The sand of the lagoon squeaks beneath my bare feet. I've always felt better touching the earth of Neverland. It knows me and I know it.

Magic likes magic.

If only I had all of mine.

None of this has gone the way it was supposed to.

"It's getting worse," Vane admits as I fall into step beside him.

"So what is the solution?" I ask because it's always better to focus on the action than it is the emotion.

"I don't know." He shakes his head, takes another pull from the cigarette, then blows out the smoke. "It was a means to an end, me claiming the shadow. I never had a plan beyond my revenge." He glances over at me with his good eye. "It wants to return to its land. I can feel it."

I don't like where this conversation is going. "So will you give it what it wants?"

"I don't want to go back to that place."

I'm relieved.

Tinkerbell was once my best friend. Murdering her left a void. Vane filled it, but there was always a glare of impermanence to it. I've always known he'll likely need to leave. A shadow belongs to a land, not the man who possesses it.

I just hoped that when he left, it would be later. Much, much later.

"You could give it back," I tell him. "Give it to someone from your island."

He glances at me again. "I won't claim the Neverland Death Shadow, if that's what you're hinting at."

I scoff. "Don't speak in such absolutes."

"You fucker. I knew that's what you were thinking."

"Vane—"

"No. If I get rid of *this* shadow, I will have unburdened myself of a disease that destroys and consumes." He points at his black eye. "Right now I can feel it swimming under the surface like the spirits of the lagoon. But unlike them, mine wants to watch pretty little girls cry while it buries its cock in their wet cunts."

He shudders at his words.

He's not just talking about *any* girl.

When the cigarette is spent, he flicks it into the lagoon and the embers fizzle out. The magic makes it disappear entirely. Gone like it never was.

"Fine, then," I say. "Get rid of the shadow and be as you were. You must have power beyond it, otherwise you wouldn't have been able to claim it."

He frowns at me. This is a subject we've never broached, but one I've always wondered about. An ordinary man cannot claim a shadow.

He shakes his head, setting his boundaries. I didn't think it would be that easy to pry out his secrets, but it was certainly worth a shot.

"How long do you think you have?" I ask instead.

"Long enough to get through this shit show, I suppose."

"All right. Then I need a few favors."

He eyes me warily. "Why do I get the distinct sense I will hate these favors?"

I ignore him. "The first favor is I need you to go to Hook and ask for his permission to enter his land."

"And what will I tell him is the reason?"

"Tell him I seem to have misplaced a Lost Boy. That'll buy us some time."

"And the second?"

I hesitate because I know he will not like this one and I'm not entirely sure I like it. But what was it Vane said? It is a means to an end.

"How would you feel about calling your brother here?" I ask.

"The fuck for? You really want me to kick that hornet's nest?"

"Oh, come on, Vane. You know your brother favors no one except for you."

He snorts. "I haven't spoken to him in years. Not since he helped us last."

"Which is why I need him again. Think of him like an insurance policy. A plan B."

"You don't call in my brother as a Plan B. And besides, last time the price was right. What the fuck would you offer him now?"

I try to keep my face impassive, but Vane knows me better than most. He meets my eyes, narrows his gaze. "Oh, I see, you asshole. You have a secret. Out with it."

I *have* been sitting on something for a very long time. It wasn't something that had any use to me, but now I think it might have doubled in value if it gets me what I want.

"Wendy Darling never went home."

"Shut the fuck up."

I say nothing. He takes several steps back to me. "Where did she go?"

"I meant to take her back. The journey didn't go as planned. And somewhere along the way I took a wrong turn."

Vane cocks his head. "And?"

"And, we ended up in Everland."

"*No*."

"*Yes*."

"And you left her?"

"More like she was liberated from my possession."

"Fucking hell." He turns a circle and scrubs at his face. "Why would you do that?"

"She was of no use to me."

"Pan!"

"Don't try to wring guilt from me. You will be left wanting. The fact remains—I know where she is and I suspect once your brother finds out she's in the realms and not bones in mortal soil, he'll want to know where, too."

"He'll fucking kill you. You know that, right?"

I snort and light my own cigarette, letting the smoke burn in my lungs before I exhale it. "I'm not worried about your brother."

"Always a cocky motherfucker, aren't you?"

"Yes." I smile at him.

He shakes his head and starts walking again. "And what is the reason I'd tell my brother to return to Neverland?"

"Tell him we need help with Captain Hook."

"Dangling two carrots in front of him, are we?"

"A king should always have carrots well stocked."

"I think it's a bad idea."

"Most good ideas start as bad ones."

He keeps walking. "I caution you against this one. Wait. Sit on it. I'm sure I can find him quickly if the need arises."

"Vane—"

"*Wait*," he says again and comes to a stop. "I beg of you."

There are very few people who I won't push to get what I want. Vane is one of them.

"Fine."

Satisfied with this, Vane trudges off again and we soon reach the base of Marooner's Rock. Vane looks up at the cliff highlighted in the glow of the moonlight. When I chased after him, I knew where he was going. When he's on edge, he loves two things to help him settle—flying and swimming in the lagoon.

He's deep in thought now, but I can tell he wants to say something. I'm not a patient man, but I let him have his minute.

"You wanted to break her," I guess. "But you didn't."

He sighs. "I will, though. If she lets me."

"No, you won't. But you will give in to her."

He scowls at me. "Is that an order?"

"It's a prediction."

"Is that so?"

"Yes. You'll give in to her because there is no other choice and because you want to."

He shakes his head and starts up the flat side of Marooner's Rock. "She annoys me and I hate her."

I follow after him. "*Wanting* her annoys you. And *hate* is just an inch away from *like*. The line is incredibly thin."

He trudges up as the hill grows steeper. "I don't know what the fuck she wants from me."

"Then ask her."

"Like you've ever asked her what she wants."

"I am a king. I don't ask, I tell. And that is what she needs from me, so that is what I give her. What she needs from you will be different and you need to figure that out before you take something she can't give."

He says nothing, which tells me he's accepted that I'm right. Because, of course, I'm right. I always am.

"And the twins?" he says over his shoulder. "What does she get from them?

"Fuck if I know what she gets from those fuckers."

He stops halfway up as the wind cuts in and dishevels his hair. "I know what it is."

"Then tell me."

"The twins take care of her in a way no one ever has."

I nod and look out over the lagoon down below. From this vantage point, the water is like a bright jewel inset in the dark, twining forest. I thought by now I would have my shadow so I could once again feel the spirits in the lagoon and the wolves in the woods and the energy in the air and the ground pulsing with life.

There is still a void and I feel empty.

A seed of doubt takes root, but I quickly banish it.

"That's another problem we need to deal with," Vane says. "The twins."

"I know."

"They're meant to be kings."

"Yes, I know that too."

"And right now there are two shadows loose on the island."

Do I trust the fae princes? They've always listened to me, even before they were banished. I was an ally of the fae court once upon a time. We were a united front against the pirates who arrived on our shores looking to steal what we had already earned.

But then Tink turned on me and the fae king followed her lead. Tilly has always pretended to be an ally and sometimes I even believed her. Clearly, I'd been a fool.

The princes hunger for home and they are desperate for their wings.

Desperate enough to turn on me?

I don't think they are disloyal, but I've been tricked before. Tricked by their own mother, who I loved like a sister, whom I gave everything I had to give. Which, it turns out, was not enough.

One problem at a time.

If only I had fewer problems.

9

WINNIE

I COME BACK TO REALITY WHEN THE COOL NIGHT AIR TICKLES THE fine hair along my temple. I'm swaying, ropes creaking. And not far off to my right is the ocean. It's so close, I can feel the dampness of the spray on my exposed skin, can taste the saltiness on the tip of my tongue.

"You with us, Darling?" Kas's voice rumbles behind me and it takes me a second to realize we're in the rope hammocks down by the water's edge and Kas is beneath me, holding me to him.

He's warm and solid and real.

He brings his hand up and is gentle with his touch as he runs his fingers through my hair.

"I'm here," I mutter, voice still muzzy with sleep.

Was I sleeping?

I can't remember, but the last stretch of time is foggy in my head.

It's the dull ache in my foot that reminds me of what happened.

Vane. The cut. The twins giving me an illusion to ease the pain as Pan stitched me up.

"Why are we in the hammocks?" I ask as it sways beneath me.

"Fresh air will do you good," Bash says from the second hammock. "And it was getting stuffy in the house. Much cooler down here."

Maybe too cool. If it wasn't for Kas wrapped around me, I might be covered in goosebumps. As it is, my legs are chilled, so I readjust, twining mine in his. He's wearing shorts, like usual, so his heat is close and immediately soothing.

I'm happy here in his arms. Content.

"Pan and Vane?" I ask and stare up at the moon.

"Pan went to check on Vane," Bash answers. "I'm sure they're fine."

I get a flash of Vane dominating me, his hand wrapped around my throat, and I clench up, the muscles tightening along my inner thighs.

My foot is aching from the cut, but my throat is throbbing more. I'm sure I'm bruised. Vane wanted to give in to his desires. I could see it in his black, black eyes.

So why didn't he? And am I glad he didn't? Or disappointed?

I should be glad.

I must be glad.

Right?

"How are you, Darling?" Kas asks and lets his fingers tickle up my forearm. I shiver beneath his attention.

The feeling I have right now reminds me of early winter mornings when the world is dark and cold, but you're sitting fireside, a cup of cocoa in hand and a blanket wrapped around your shoulders.

I've had that just once in my life and it is the most vivid memory I have because it ached, how good it felt.

"I'm okay," I answer.

"Vane shouldn't have come at you like that," Bash says.

"It's okay. Really."

Kas sighs into my hair. "No, it's not."

I'm starting to see the lines drawn between the boys. Pan and Vane are a lot alike. Both brutal and unforgiving and so vicious it makes your teeth hurt.

The twins are more merciful, but intentionally devilish because they enjoy it.

I like them all for different reasons, in different ways.

And yes, even Vane.

Even the Dark One with his brutality.

When I finally get him all to myself, I'm absolutely sure it will be an event I will not soon forget.

Beyond our little grove, I hear footsteps crack a few fallen twigs on the path. The twins don't seem concerned, so neither am I.

It's Cherry who comes up a few seconds later.

"Hi," she says.

"What do you want?" Bash asks.

"I haven't seen you guys in a while. Is everything all right?"

Kas tenses up beneath me.

Maybe she's fishing for details? I honestly don't know the Cherry story, but I'm definitely curious about it. I get the impression none of them want her here, but they can't get rid of her either, despite their lack of care when it comes to the lives of those around them.

Why is that?

"I heard Pan yelling earlier," she goes on. "And then I saw all the broken glass. What happened?"

"Pan lost his—" I start, but Bash cuts me off.

"Lost his shit. You know how he gets."

Cherry crosses her arms over her chest and glances at me. I try not to look like I know more than I should.

"Winnie?" she says.

"I'm just here for the ride," I mutter.

Kas's hand wraps around my bicep and gives me an appreciative squeeze.

So they don't want her to know the details of what happened?

"Where's Vane?" she asks next, keeping her voice intentionally level.

Bash lifts his hand, pointing a finger at the sky.

Cherry takes several steps down to the beach and stops, gaze pointed toward the clouds.

"What is she—" And that's when I see it, a dark shape flying through the clouds.

"Is that Vane?" I disentangle myself from Kas and the hammock wobbles.

"Christ," Kas says and quickly plants his feet to the sand to steady us. "Give me a warning next time, Darling."

"Sorry." Once I'm out of the rope hammock, I hurry down the beach to Cherry's side.

"It's incredible, isn't it?" she says, never taking her eyes off the dark figure darting through the clouds.

"Is that really him?" I ask.

"Mmmhmmm. He's one of the only ones on the island, other than the royal fae, who can fly."

I'm entranced by him, by his nimble flight, the way he dips and turns and then disappears into a tall, fluffy cloud only to burst out the other side.

"He flies when he's angry," Cherry explains, pride

leaking into her voice. She knows something I don't and she's happy to rub it in.

"If I could fly, I'd use any excuse to do it."

The twins join us on the beach, one on either side of us. They watch Vane too, but I catch a different emotion on Bash's face—*jealousy*.

They had wings once. Just like their sister. I don't know how they lost them, but I can tell it cost them something.

Both of the boys are shirtless, their straight-lined tattoos standing out against their dark skin. But when I lean back and inspect their shoulders, there's no trace of wings there. No scars or stumps. Nothing to hint that they once had fairy wings and could fly like Vane.

Several seagulls cry from the shore, but our attention is still locked on Vane.

He zips in front of the full moon then turns on his back. His body goes limp and he starts to fall.

"Hey," I say and take a step forward. "Is that normal? Should he be doing that?"

His arms and legs are held out as he falls.

The closer he gets to the ground, the faster he seems to fall.

"Kas? Bash? Shouldn't he be doing something?"

Kas hooks his arm around my shoulder and tugs me into his side. "Just watch, Darling."

My heart kicks up as Vane falls and falls, the ground rushing up to greet him. I hold my breath. What the hell is he doing? If he hits the ground, he'll—

At the last second, he rolls and darts back up, taking off like a rocket.

I exhale in a rush. "Goddamn him."

"He knew we were watching," Cherry says, her voice lilting. "He was just showing off."

Bash snorts. "For you, maybe. I don't have a hard-on for the Dark One."

Checking Cherry beside me, it's hard not to miss the glitter in her eyes. Her hands are clasped at her chest as she watches Vane and I'm all of a sudden envious of her. She's had him. I haven't.

Vane sails for the ground once again, but he's very clearly in control this time and lands with a soft thud ten yards off from us.

He is a dark figure as he makes his way up the beach.

Cherry is giddy.

When Vane comes into a slant of moonlight, his cheeks are ruddy, his hair windswept. Somehow, he's sexier than he's ever been.

Maybe it's because he looks relaxed. Happy even.

And then he opens his mouth. "The fuck are you all looking at?"

"As if you don't know," Bash says and turns away, climbs back into a hammock.

"That was so awesome." Cherry bounces on the pads of her feet. "Like absolutely amazing."

Vane runs his hand through his hair, raking it back. "I have a job for you, Cherry."

"Okay! Sure. What is it?"

He pushes past us and doesn't even look at me and my stomach hits my feet.

"I need to speak to your brother," he says, "and I want you with me."

Cherry deflates. "I'd really rather not—"

"It wasn't a suggestion," he says over his shoulder. "We'll leave in fifteen minutes."

"Wait..." I sidle up next to Cherry. "Who's your brother?"

All of her excitement has drained away as she watches Vane stalk up the hill to the house.

"Hook," she tells me with a bite to her words. "Captain James Hook."

10

CHERRY

I don't want to return to James's side of the island but I'll never pass up the opportunity to have Vane all to myself.

He gave me fifteen minutes to get ready, so I'm going to spend every single one of those minutes making sure I look cute and enticing.

When my brother gave me to Pan and the Lost Boys, I sobbed for days in the tiny room where they stuck me. It's at the end of one of the hallways on the main floor. Far, far away from the loft. That was several years ago now. It feels like a lifetime. Like I've always been here in Pan's house, the only girl amongst the Lost Boys.

Well...until Winnie.

I don't hate this Darling like I thought I would. But I don't like her either.

All of the boys are tripping over themselves to have her. I'm not sure why. Her boobs aren't as big as mine and she's rail thin.

But she is nice. So I have to give her that.

I just don't want to have to compete with her for Vane. I've spent the last several years trying to get his attention. I've done everything short of bowing at his feet and worshipping the ground he walks on.

I'd have done that too if he'd let me.

But then...he finally gave in.

I shudder at the memory.

I'm okay with getting the worst of Vane if I can have any of him at all.

My body still aches from the... Pounding is the only word. Even if it is inadequate.

I'm still sore between my legs and bruises still pepper my skin. I wear them proudly, of course.

I have the marks of his hands on my skin. Winnie Darling just has a bruise around her throat from when she made him mad.

In my room, I put on my best dress, one I bought with my own money from a dress shop in Darlington. It's deep indigo with a low-cut neckline and a pleated skirt. In the mirror over my dresser, I check my reflection and smooth over my hair.

Does Vane like my hair up or down? I suppose if it's up, he can get a better look at *my* neck. I'm more than happy to let him choke me.

My inner walls tighten at the thought.

Before I leave my room, I decide to leave my panties behind.

Who knows how Vane will feel after we leave my brother's. If Hook is anything like he used to be, he'll piss Vane off and he'll need to expend some of that energy.

And I'll be more than happy to help.

Vane is silent as we leave the house on foot. We follow the road toward town and skirt the perimeter, keeping away from the busier heart of Darlington. Everyone will fawn over Vane if they see him. He's smart to take the lesser traveled roads.

"Why are we going to my brother?" I finally dare to ask.

Vane's longer legs keep a quicker pace than my shorter ones so I have to fast-walk next to him.

"Pan needs permission to enter his territory."

"Why?"

"Why do you ask so many questions?"

"That's only two."

"That's two too many."

We keep walking. Frogs croak in the marshy land to the left of the road and moonlight gleams on the brackish water. It stinks in this part of Neverland. Like lit matches and moldy flowers.

Vane lights a cigarette and the burning tobacco takes some of the stench away.

"So...is Winnie staying on the island for a while?" I ask.

Vane blows smoke. "Fuck if I know."

"Do you want her to?"

He stops all of a sudden and I slip on the graveled road when I overcorrect to come back to him.

"Cherry, listen to me very carefully."

I nod, trying to focus, but he's so nice to look at, it's hard to think of anything other than his mouth on me.

"Cherry." He snaps his fingers.

"I'm listening."

"I don't want to speak on this trip. No talking at all. Not a single fucking word. Can you do that?"

"Ummm..." That doesn't sound very fun. "Not even—"

"Not. One. Word."

"But—"

"For fuck's sake." He grumbles to himself and surges ahead again.

I chase after him.

"Vane?" He doesn't respond. "Vane?" I say again.

"What?" he barks.

"Do you like her?"

Please say no. Please say no.

He scowls at me and I shiver beneath his glimmering black eye. "Cherry."

"Yes?"

"Shut the fuck up."

11

CAPTAIN JAMES HOOK

The fae queen's handwriting is elegant and slanted on the creased parchment paper.

The words leave a taste in my mouth, though I don't know if it's bitter or pleasant.

Let us unite against Peter Pan, the queen has said. *As we were meant to.*

Just the mere suggestion of it has my blood boiling. We were supposed to align once upon a time. We were supposed to be rid of Peter Pan too.

Conjuring an image of the Never King makes my residual limb ache.

Every time I think about him, I shake with rage.

I turn back to the letter to distract myself and rub the thick paper between thumb and forefinger. It's good paper. Thick and velvety. Paper can say a lot about a man. So can his handwriting. His clothing. His posture. His diction. I suppose everything can say a lot about a man. And a fae queen too.

She closes the letter with, *And I can help you defend your-self against the Crocodile, should he return to the island.*

If I hate Peter Pan, my feelings on the Crocodile are ten times worse. I'm not sure there is a word in the dictionary that would suffice for what I feel for the Crocodile.

Sometimes when I lie in bed, I can see him in my mind's eye.

The hard lines of his body. The sharp teeth.

A chill fills the room and I'm not sure if it's the ocean breeze or the sensation of my own rage borne to life.

Folding the letter again, I set it neatly beside my quill and go to the window and look out on the bay where my ship is moored in the night. The moonlight finds its masts and makes it glow against the twilight sky.

A man's ship and the way it's kept says more than paper, and the Jolly Roger says that I am a man who deserves respect. Even on an island full of magic and duplicitous bastards.

Even—

Somewhere beyond my study, I hear the ticking of a clock.

It's pitiful, the way my heart seizes up and my stomach clenches.

It's pitiful that the sound of a ticking clock makes me see nothing but a beast in my mind's eye, the way his tongue lapped up my blood.

I leave the room, stalk down the hall, and enter the front parlor. My men are drinking and cavorting. We haven't been at sea in several months and it's starting to show. They're drunk and rowdy and filthy. Several are in the middle of a poker game, chips strewn over the sticky table.

The ticking is so loud in my head, I swear I can hear it in my bones.

I spot a pocket watch amongst the betting pile on the green felt table and stalk toward it. Several men take notice and go quiet, and the ticking grows louder making my eye twitch and my hand ache.

No, not my hand.

My hook.

When I reach the table, the players gaze up at me, blinking. "Hi, Captain," the man on my left says. "Did you care to join the game? We could—"

I cock my arm back and then slam my hook down on the watch. The glass shatters and the clock face crumbles beneath the force.

My hook has gone straight through the table and it takes me several yanks to spring it free.

The watch stays pierced on the curved tine of my hook.

I look at the men sitting around the table. "Poor form. Poor form!"

"Sorry, Captain. We didn't—"

"I said no watches or clocks. None. Do you idiots know what none means? Zero. Fucking zero." I hunch, putting my face in his and he shrinks back. He stinks like cheap ale and stale cigarettes. He's missing several teeth and the sight of the gaping holes in his mouth makes me want to smash his fucking face into the table.

Do these men not know how to take care of themselves?

"Next time," I warn and hold up the hook and the smashed watch, "this will be your fucking eyeball. Do you understand?"

"Aye, Captain. Apologies, Captain."

"Jas." Smee puts her hand on my arm. "We need to talk."

My blood is boiling and I can feel the heat of it fanning in my face. Maybe I'll claim his eyeball now. Teach them all a fucking lesson.

"Jas!"

I whirl on Smee. "WHAT?"

"I need to speak with you. Right now." She yanks the pocket watch from the end of my hook and shoves me toward the study.

It isn't until we're inside, the door shut, that she frowns at me. "Poor form," she says, echoing my favorite saying.

"I said no fucking watches, Smee!"

She crosses her arms over her chest. Smee was once Samira, but at just five years old, Cherry couldn't pronounce it and Samira became Smee.

The name stuck and she let us keep it.

She comes over to me now, her long locs sliding heavily over her shoulder. "Why are you in a tiff?"

"I'm not in a fucking tiff."

The line of her brow sinks over her dark brown eyes. "You're shouting and cussing. That's a tiff."

I sigh and drop into my leather chair behind the desk. "The fae queen wrote to me."

"And?"

"And something is going on. I can feel it. She's offering an alliance—"

"Cherry is here."

I look up at her. "*What?*"

"It's why I wanted to talk to you. Clearly not a coincidence now that I know of the letter."

"What does Cherry want?"

Twice I've dared to cross the border to check on my little sister. Twice I've regretted it.

"Apparently, she's at the gate with the Dark One. They're asking for you."

"What's their reason?"

"They wouldn't give one."

I feel sick.

I don't want to see Cherry. I certainly don't want to see Cherry with the Dark One. I've heard the stories. Sometimes I regret handing her over. Sometimes I have to remind myself that she had little use for me and still doesn't.

She was always enamored with Pan and the Lost Boys. She would have turned on me eventually.

My little sister is adorable and kind until she isn't.

Which was why, when Peter Pan captured Smee in one of our endless wars, I traded Cherry for Smee's return.

Smee had always held more value than Cherry.

And in a way, Cherry being a hostage of Pan's has brokered the intended peace.

I would never endanger my sister's life so the fighting has stopped.

For the most part, of course. Pan just killed two of my men a few days ago because they crossed the boundary lines.

Poor form, indeed.

"What do you want to do?" Smee asks.

I scratch at my jaw as I think and the stubble rasps.

Something is going on and I want to know what.

"Show them in," I say.

There are bruises peppering my sister's skin and the sight of it makes me ill.

What have they done to you?

I want to ask her but I'm not sure she'd answer me. How could she give me anything when I was supposed to protect her?

Besides, she may be bruised, but her eyes are bright as she stands proudly next to the Dark One.

No one ages on Neverland, but somehow Cherry looks older. She got our mother's thick, dark red hair. We both have her freckles, but Cherry got more than I did and mine have dulled beneath the sun.

I've thought of this moment for years. Gone over in my head what I'd say to her when we had the chance to finally speak. But now that she's in front of me, I have no comforting words to offer her.

I gave her up to the enemy. And while it's a common practice where we came from, it was never something that sat well with me. Even if I still believe to this day that it was the right decision to make.

"Sit," I tell them once they're in my study. "Can I offer you a drink?"

"No," Vane says as he takes the leather chair that sits in front of my desk. Cherry follows his lead and sits beside him. It makes my skin crawl.

"All right," I say and sit. "To what do I owe the pleasure?"

"We seem to have lost one of our Lost Boys," Vane says. "Pan would like your permission to enter your territory to look for him."

Lies.

I sit forward and put my elbow to the desk, letting my hook take center stage. Vane pays it no mind. Cherry can't take her eyes off the pointy tine.

She was just a kid when the Crocodile took my hand. Perhaps she can remember the screaming. The blood.

I swallow hard against the bile rising up my throat.

I detest the sight of my own blood.

"I suppose a Lost Boy is apt to get lost," I say.

"Indeed," Vane answers.

I don't like dealing with the Dark One. I like it even less than dealing with Pan. The sooner I can get him out of my house the better.

His face reminds me of familiar things. Things I'd rather forget.

"Suppose I allow Pan to cross the boundary," I say. "What do I get in return?"

Vane doesn't have to consider this question. He and Pan have clearly already thought of this request.

"We'll give you back your sister."

Cherry's head whips his way and her mouth drops open. She didn't know?

And why does she look like she wants to scream?

Maybe she hates me for giving her up, but surely, she'd want to come home if given the chance?

I swear I can hear the bite of her teeth.

Vane reacts not at all.

"That's it?" I ask. "No other conditions?"

"No."

"What if I don't want to come back?" Cherry barks.

Vane turns his head her way, slowly and deliberately. "You don't have a say in the matter."

"But—"

When the Dark One scowls at her, she snaps her mouth shut.

I don't blame her. I would too.

"I have some business to attend to," I say. "I'll give Peter Pan permission to enter my territory two nights from now. Let's give the Lost Boy some time to turn up on his own. How does that sound?"

Vane's smile is tight against his teeth, more sinister than mine, and it makes the hair at the nape of my neck stand upright. "Fine," Vane says. "In two nights." He pushes off of the chair and turns for the door, snapping his fingers at Cherry as he leaves.

"And my sister?" I ask.

Cherry barely looks at me.

Vane glances over his shoulder. "Pan will bring her to you in three nights."

Cherry's frown deepens. I'm not sure if I can convince her to stay. But I'll try my damnedest.

"Very well."

When they're gone, I pull open the bottom drawer on my desk and fetch my bottle of Caribbean rum. There are two glasses there too and I pull out both, knowing Smee isn't far off.

She appears a handful of minutes after I've poured us each a glass.

"So?" she says and takes the rum in hand.

"I think Peter Pan found his shadow," I say.

Smee arches a brow.

"And I think it's here on my side of the island."

Smee sits in the chair Vane just inhabited. She spreads out her long legs and crosses them at the ankle. "That explains the fae queen's letter."

I point a finger at her. "Precisely."

We drink in silence as I consider my options. When the glass is empty, I start moving.

"Do you have a plan?" Smee asks as she follows me back out to the parlor.

"Yes." To the men I say, "On your feet."

Smee comes up beside me. Her dark skin stands out against the creamy white of her button-up shirt. She's cast off the jacquard vest, has her sleeves rolled up to her elbows. She smells like lavender and tallow soap. Her stomach groans. Smee could eat all day long and always be starving. I'm not sure where she puts it. She's always been lean and lithe.

"What are you doing?" she whispers to me.

"Gentlemen, I need you to scour my territory. Start at the border and work your way back to the bay."

"What are we looking for?" one of the burly men asks.

"Excellent question." I clasp my hands behind my back and pace to the bar. "I'm looking for a shadow." I turn on my heel and face them. "Peter Pan's shadow, to be exact."

I offer the men a twenty pence reward if they find the shadow and once there's money on the table, they're all but stumbling over themselves to get out the door.

Smee and I watch them from the leaded glass windows as they race down the road toward the border.

"What are you doing, Jas?" Smee asks.

"If I have Peter Pan's shadow," I say, "then I won't have to worry about the Crocodile. Or the fae queen. Two birds, one stone."

"And what happens to Cherry if you claim the shadow before she's been returned?"

I look over at her. "If I have the shadow, there will be nothing Peter Pan can do to stop me."

12

WELL INTO THE MIDDLE OF THE NIGHT, THE TWINS DECIDE TO GO for a run because apparently that's something they do often. Vane and Cherry have returned from their mission, but Vane is in a bad mood and so is Cherry, though their bad moods are the difference between chocolate and a volcano.

I decide it's best to leave them both alone and wander the halls of the house looking for something to occupy my time. Pan must be here somewhere.

I find a separate set of stairs just beyond the entrance to his tomb and there's a distinct sound coming from above, like someone is riffling through things.

I go up.

Peter Pan is there, pulling open drawers in a large cabinet. His back is to me, but I'm absolutely sure he's immediately aware that I'm there.

"What are you looking for?" I ask.

"Something to draw my shadow to me." He digs inside

another drawer. "I need a tether or I will be endlessly chasing the damn thing."

"And that tether is here?"

"I'm not sure. Possibly." He slams the drawer shut and yanks open another.

This room is at the top of the tower and has a large circular window to match the one in the library. Except this one is nearly at floor level so when I go to it, it feels like I'm looking through a portal into another world.

The ocean is painted in silver strokes of moonlight. To the north is the craggy cliff of Marooner's Rock. And from this height, I can make out some of the glowing swirls in the turquoise lagoon.

I jump when another drawer slams shut.

"Is Vane all right?" I ask.

I look over my shoulder to find Pan facing me. "Honestly? I'm not sure." He goes to a little end table beside a wingback chair and yanks open the single drawer in it.

"Did I do something wrong?" I ask and skirt the room. "Tell me how I should be around Vane."

I've always prided myself on being able to figure people out. But Vane is an exception and it's frustrating me beyond reason.

Pan pauses in his search. "I'm not sure there is a way to be around Vane." He returns to digging.

"Has he always been like that?"

"Ruthless? Prickly? Yes."

"Is it just the way he is or the shadow?"

"I wouldn't know. I didn't know him before he'd claimed it."

"And he's not from this island?"

"No." He goes to a tall desk shoved beneath a run of bookshelves and upends a metal box. Several papers and trinkets fall out, but not what he's looking for, apparently.

"Where does he come from?"

"Another island."

"Yes, but which one? Cherry said there were seven?"

"Cherry talks too much." He yanks a book from the shelf and holds it up by its spine and gives it a shake.

I think back on what Vane told me about his island, how it breaks girls like me for no good reason other than to watch them crack.

And I'm sick of it, he'd said.

The way he'd held me that night…

Just thinking about it makes my entire body tremble and my stomach fill with butterflies.

I don't know how to reconcile that Vane with the same Vane that bruised my throat and held me against the wall.

Not that I mind him being rough with me.

But how far does his shadow have to take it? What is the line and what happens if he crosses it?

Pan tosses a book to the floor, grabs another.

"Pan?"

"Yes, Darling?"

"Is Vane sleeping with Cherry?" I try to keep my voice light, but it's dripping with jealousy.

He stops searching for this magical mystery object and looks over at me. "The Death Shadow needs to chase something. It needs to spend its energy. If it doesn't, it'll start killing things."

"That doesn't answer my question."

"He was," he says. "I'm not sure if he still is."

"I meant what I said. I don't want to share any of you."

"I'm not sure you can make that condition with Vane." He plucks a third book, gives it a shake, and tosses it.

"How do I get to him?"

He tosses the next book and the one after that.

"Pan."

He finally stops. "You want to know how to get to the Dark One? Stop trying." He resumes his search.

I'm not sure if Pan knows it or not, but I feel like he's just given me the secret codex for Vane.

It makes so much sense now.

Of course someone like Vane hates when someone tries too hard and I've been throwing myself at him. Cherry has been doing the same thing and Vane can barely stand her.

God, I've been so stupid.

From now on, he's getting my cold shoulder. So cold it'll burn.

Pan grabs a thick leather-bound book and thumbs through its pages and comes to an abrupt stop.

"Did you find it?" I ask him, slightly curious as to what this thing is.

He comes over to the desk and drops the book, lets it flop open to reveal a cut out in the pages. "I don't remember putting this here, but I am forgetful these days."

There's a smooth black seashell inside the hideaway.

"Is that it?"

"That's it." He plucks the shell out. Its body is curled in on itself like a wave.

"It doesn't look special."

"It's from the lagoon."

"Oh?"

"Your mother gave it to me."

I frown up at him. "Really? How did she come to possess a magical seashell?"

He grabs my hand and opens it up, setting the shell inside the cup of my palm. It's much warmer than I would have expected and holding it makes my skin tingle. "How old was your mother when she had you?" he asks.

The way he says it, it doesn't sound like a curiosity. More like a trivia question.

"Nineteen," I answer.

He nods. "Remember me telling you I took her to the lagoon after Tilly got inside her head? That she was in pain and that I'd hoped the lagoon would help soothe her?"

Of course I remember. It was the first time I realized Peter Pan had a heart.

"Yes," I answer.

"I took her because she was worried."

"About what?"

"About the baby in her womb. About *you*."

13

PETER PAN

It wasn't until after Merry's first encounter with the fae queen that she admitted she was pregnant.

She'd clutched at me, sobbing, and said, "Please save my baby. I don't want to die here."

There had always been something about Merry that made us all act differently.

She'd been like a little sister from the first moment she arrived on the island.

We hated to watch her suffer. I, especially, hated to watch her suffer.

She'd waded into the waters of the lagoon and floated on the turquoise surface on her back as swirls of light filled the air around her.

"Better?" I'd called out to her.

"Much," she'd said.

She stayed there for hours, and I sat on the shore watching her and the light, wondering if I had it all wrong, if it was time to give up my pursuit.

When Merry waded back out, she'd held a seashell in her hand. "Where did you get that?" I'd asked.

The lagoon never gave up its treasures despite many men trying. There were several dead pirates at the bottom of the water, men who'd dove in and tried to take what they had not earned.

Merry looked down at her hand and frowned. "I don't know. Maybe...*oh*." Her gaze had gone far away like she'd been listening to something beyond my comprehension. "Treasure," she'd said. "For you." And then she handed it over and as soon as the shell was in my grip, I knew immediately it was magic.

And now the dark object sits in Darling's hand over eighteen years later.

"My mom...was pregnant on the island?" she asks.

I drop into the wingback chair, suddenly exhausted. The sun is coming. Much quicker than I'd like.

"She was indeed," I answer.

"She never told me."

There is a matching chair across from me and Darling sits on the edge of the seat. "That means...in a way...that I was here before."

"I suppose you're right."

Perhaps that's why, when she's in my arms, I feel like I've come home.

I will never tell her that.

I will not tell a soul.

I don't have weaknesses and certainly not pretty little Darling girls.

"When I first came to the island," she says, "it immediately felt familiar. Is that possible?"

"Anything is possible on Neverland."

She turns back to the seashell and scrutinizes it more closely. "This almost feels like it's buzzing."

The fact that she can feel the magic in the shell is concerning, though not surprising.

"You really think this will help you get your shadow?" she asks.

"If I am this island's beating heart," I tell her, "then the lagoon is its soul. I don't remember anything of my life before I arrived here. My first memory is of the lagoon. And one thing I know for certain is that whatever it spits out is always full of magic. So yes, I do."

My skin is beginning to itch.

"I need to get below ground, Darling."

"Oh. Right." She gets up and brings the shell back to me. She's not wearing a bra and her nipples are pebbled beneath the material. The soft golden light of the lantern behind her limns her in gold.

I grab her by the wrist and yank her into my lap. She lets out a little yelp.

"Come to bed with me," I tell her.

She wiggles on my lap and my cock takes notice.

"Ask me nicely."

A rumble starts in my chest. I wrap my hand around the back of her neck and drag her ear to my mouth. "Come to bed with me, my little Darling whore, so I can shove my cock in your wet cunt and make you beg for mercy."

An exhale rushes past her wet lips and she presses her thighs together.

I bring my other hand up her bare leg, up her thigh, and the air gets stuck in her throat.

She makes a soft hiccupping noise as my fingers stop just a few inches from her pussy.

I swear I can feel the heat of her.

"What if I'm not tired?" she challenges.

Naughty girl.

"We could start with a bath." I slide closer to her center and she parts her thighs for me. "You are filthy, after all."

She laughs on a breath. "I'm full of Peter Pan's cum."

"Mmm. Just the way I like you."

And I do. I fucking do. I want her pumped full of my cum every fucking day.

The sun creeps closer to the horizon, but I'm suddenly in no rush.

I bring my fingers to the flat plane of her panties and ghost over the wet material. She hisses and bucks against me, but I still have my other hand wrapped around the back of her throat. She's not going anywhere. Not yet anyway.

"Come to bed with me," I tell her again. "Say yes, Darling."

I slide over her clit and apply just enough pressure to make her squirm.

"All right."

That's all I need to hear. I lift her off of me, setting her feet to the floor. "Hurry, Darling." She rushes ahead of me to the tower and down, down the stairwell.

The sun may be rising, but as long as I'm in darkness, I can manage another hour or two.

Long enough to make Darling scream my name.

14

WINNIE

As he promised, Pan draws a bath and I circle his room while he does.

This is the space that is most *him*.

The walls are painted a dark emerald green that reminds me of the green of the Neverland forest. The giant four-poster bed is covered in a charcoal gray linen duvet that is ridiculously sumptuous between my fingers.

In the corner, there's the wingback and a table and lamp. The dresser with trinkets displayed on top. A little fairy carved from beach wood. A fossil. A delicate skeleton leaf trapped in a glass jar.

As the water fills the tub, I scan the books stacked up around the perimeter of the room. Some of them aren't labeled and it's those that I suspect might be journals, and the urge to flip one open and read Peter Pan's deepest, darkest thoughts is overwhelming.

But I don't.

I wouldn't dare.

Shoved in amongst the journals are old leather-bound books with spines that look like ribs. *Brave New World.* *Lord of the Flies. Crime and Punishment.* Even *Pride and Prejudice.*

I love that he and Vane read so much.

"Get in here, Darling," he calls from the bathroom once the tap has been shut off.

I cross the room and poke my head in through the cracked doorway. Pan's bathroom is big and carved from stone. Several wrought iron lanterns flicker with light from their hooks embedded in the walls.

Pan stands beside the deep, wide tub as steam ribbons around his naked body.

Holy good god.

His cock is fully erect, his balls taut against his body.

As he breathes, his abs contract, shadowing the deep lines between each muscle.

He's already dipped his hand into the water and raked his fingers through his hair so that it sticks up in the most roguish way.

Two minutes ago, I was overwhelmed with the urge to riffle through his books. Now I'm overwhelmed with the urge to run my hands over his naked body.

He comes over to me and his cock digs into my belly and my pussy tingles at the obsceneness of it all.

"Arms up," he commands and I do as he says. He lifts my dress off and as soon as my breasts hit the air, my nipples tighten and he takes in the sight of me with those bright blue eyes of his, causing a shiver to roll down my spine.

"Off," he says.

There's only one piece of clothing left on my body, so I don't need a hint as to what he means. I hook my fingers into the waistband of my panties and slide them off and step out of them.

He offers me his hand and when I take it, he helps me over the rim of the tub. The water is warm and smells like Pan, like summer nights and dark secrets. There is a slight, sharp burn at the cut on my foot as soon as I hit the water, but the pain quickly fades.

Pan climbs in on the other side and the water rises up to meet him. He props his arms on his knees. Beads of water run down his biceps, following the curve of muscle.

I don't think I will ever be quenched of my thirst for Peter Pan.

He reaches across the tub, grabs my wrist, and yanks me into him.

A short exhale escapes me as he turns my back into his chest and nestles me between his legs. His hardness presses against me and a tingle of anticipation pools in my clit.

"Do you take baths with all the girls on the island?" I joke because I'm suddenly nervous and excited all at the same time.

I know how to take what I need from men.

But Peter Pan is no man.

And unlike anyone I've ever met.

He is a mirage I am endlessly chasing and I'm terrified of both reaching him and never reaching him.

Beneath the surface of the water, he wraps his arms around my waist.

"Only the filthy ones." His voice is rough and ragged at my ear as his hand drifts up, his thumb grazing the sensitive underside of my breast.

Despite the heat of the water, I'm still pebbled, desperate for his touch.

His other hand goes in the opposite direction, stopping once he's reached my inner thigh.

I breathe out excitedly.

His fingers ghost further up and I tremble in anticipation.

He leaves my breast and I whimper with the loss, until his hand wraps around my throat and forces my chin up.

"Did you like being used tonight, Darling?"

I pant out my response. "Yes. Maybe more than I should."

"I want you to be our good girl and take our cocks whenever we'd like."

My clit throbs beneath his words.

"I can do that."

"Can you?"

"Yes."

"I want you always full of our cum like a good little whore. Do you understand, Darling?"

I whimper as his hand tightens around my throat. "Yes."

"That's my good girl." He ends the torture and slides his fingers down my slit. I whimper and buck, but he holds me fast.

My clit is throbbing and somehow he's brought me close to the edge with barely any touch at all.

"Pan," I breathe out.

"Yes, Darling?"

"Fuck me."

Without warning, he spins me around in the water and hoists me up on the stone surrounding the tub. I hiss at the sudden cold on my ass.

He reaches behind me and I quiver with anticipation. When he pulls back, there's a cloth in his hand. He gets it wet and sudsy and brings the soft fabric to my breast. The soap glides over my nipple.

My heart thumps in my throat and I swallow hard.

"Are you filthy, Darling?" he asks me.

I prop myself up on my elbows, head hung back, eyes closed. "Yes."

He goes to my other breast, teasing at the nipple before rolling it between his fingers, causing me to jolt from the ache.

I'm buzzing between my legs, so ready for him to take me.

When will he end the torture?

The cloth trails down between my breasts, down the flat plane of my stomach.

"Spread your legs for me," he orders and I do as I'm told.

He squeezes the cloth in his hand and soapy water drips over my pussy.

"Oh god," I say to the ceiling. I'm tingling so much, I worry I might come at the slightest bit of touching.

"When you are under my command, I am your god," he says.

The cloth caresses at my clit and the pleasure blooms at my core.

"Yes. Pan. Fuck."

He just barely lets the edge of the fabric tease at my opening, then up and around my clit. It's a feather touch but enough to make me tremble and damn near beg for more.

I reach over without thinking, desperate for release, but he bats my hand away.

"You are not allowed to touch," he says.

The water sloshes as he rises up on his knees. I part my lids, watching him, the muscle and tendons twining in his shoulders as he moves toward me and when he crests the surface of the water, his cock is rock hard.

He sinks forward and bends me in half, bracing the backside of my legs against his chest. His cock slides up my wet slit, the head hitting my clit. He pumps forward and back a few times, the heat of him, the touch of him, sending me careening.

"Don't stop," I say on a moan.

"As if you can tell me what to do." He hooks an arm around my thighs, caging me against him, squeezing my thighs together, creating the perfect amount of friction and tightness between us.

He rocks again and blood pounds through me as the flame flickers at my core.

"Please, Pan. Please don't stop."

He picks up the pace, fucking my clit.

The tension builds.

Sweat glistens on his forehead as water drips down his body.

"You're so fucking wet, Darling," he says.

"Yes," I pant out and squeeze my thighs harder, driving him against my clit.

"Where do you want me to come?"

"I get a choice?"

"Just this once."

"Inside of me."

He laughs above me. "That was the wrong one."

He pumps harder, faster. I want him inside of me but I don't think he'll give in to me.

Everything with Pan is always a dance between what I want and what he'll give me. And I love every fucking part of it.

"I'm close," I tell him because I don't want to come alone.

"Not yet," he says, his voice labored with his thrusts.

The pressure builds and my body tenses up, but Pan holds fast to me, keeping up the pace and the rhythm.

"Oh, fuck. Yes," I say. "Just like that." He's growing harder by the second and I can feel every ridge of him against my slickness. "I can't hold on anymore."

"Look at me, Darling," he commands. "I want to see the look in your eyes when you come all over my dick."

I pant out hard and open my eyes for him.

There's a blazing hunger in his gaze as he watches, as he pumps against me.

"Go on," he orders. "Come for me."

I couldn't hold on another second if I tried.

The wave crashes through me and I cry out, muscles and nerves blinking.

Instinctively I want to tense up, curl up, but Pan keeps me in place as he chases his own pleasure, teeth gnashed around a guttural groan.

My nerves fire and I tremble beneath him as he comes too. He comes all over me and I can feel the hot seed of Peter Pan making a mess of my clit, dripping down the center of me.

When he crashes over the other side and I stop quivering beneath him, he finally pulls back and takes in the sight of me, legs spread for the king.

"My filthy little Darling whore," he says, his voice hoarse as he catches his breath. "Just the way I like her."

15

KAS

BASH AND I LIKE TO RUN THE PERIMETER OF PAN'S TERRITORY. WE
do it nearly every day. And inevitably, when we skirt the fae
territory, our pace slows and our eyes wander.

We can't see the palace from our favorite trail, but we
can sense it through the forest.

Today we stop, panting loudly, sweat pouring down our
backs. Day has nearly broken across the sky and the
nocturnal animals of the Neverland forest have gone quiet
and still. Except for us.

"I have a question for you," Bash says, his hands on his
hips. He's pacing back and forth in front of the foot path
that leads from Pan's side of the island to our sister's land.

"I'm listening," I say and bend over so I can wind my
hair back up into a rubber band. Some days I consider
cutting it like my twin so we can be identical once again. He
cut his as soon as we were banished.

"If our family doesn't want me any longer, than I don't
want the custom," he'd said.

Long hair is a symbol of many things for the royal family—strength, virility, power, status. But to our nani, it was the infinite symbol of the island and the earth, much like the sweetgrass that grows around the palace.

"We touch the grass," Nani had said to me when I was a boy, as she'd drug her fingers through the feathered heads of the blooming stalks, "and the grass remembers. If we cut the grass, it will forget who we are and we never want the island to forget." She'd turned to me then and patted the top of my head. "The same is said for our hair. It is a physical manifestation of our memories and our experiences. We touch our hair with our fingers and we will remember who we are."

She died when Bash and I were just seven years old.

Sometimes I wonder what our life would be like if she'd lived longer.

Course, Nani hated our mother too. If Pan hadn't killed Tink, Nani might have eventually.

Nani didn't like that our father married a common house fae.

"Did you get the sense," Bash says now, "that our dear sister was plotting when she came to the loft? Not the part where she tried to scramble our Darling's brain. Something else. Something beyond that."

I straighten and sweat drips down my forehead. I swipe it away with the backside of my hand. "Maybe," I admit. "She seemed far too eager to get her hands on the Darling's head."

"That exactly." Bash's hands are on his hips as he turns a circle and thinks. "How much you want to bet she already knows Pan's shadow has returned to the island?"

"I only bet what I know I can win."

Bash nods.

I've been thinking about our sister a lot lately. About her lies. About our truths.

Does she know why Bash and I killed our father?

Could she ever forgive us and allow us to come home?

It's hard not to tether myself to the hope that she might change her mind. The hope is the buoy and I've treading water for too long, the sea dragging me out.

I can't let it go.

I won't.

But Darling has changed things.

For one, our sister was going to scramble her mind just like she did Merry's. She knew what she was doing and she did it anyway.

And two...

If we leave Peter Pan and the Treehouse, we leave Darling. Pan would never let us take her with us. The thought of that makes my shoulders knot up and my stomach twist.

Beyond all that...Tilly hasn't felt like my sister for a very long time and I don't know how to grapple with that feeling.

When I look at her, it's like looking at a stranger. Is it that we've changed and she hasn't? That we've become something dark and untenable?

Or is it the distance between us? If we went home, would that change? Would proximity breed familiarity and all would be well again?

I stop at the mouth of the path home. It's overgrown now. There aren't many who travel back and forth between Pan's land and Tilly's. Not since he killed Tink and we were banished.

"I have an idea," I say.

"A good idea or a bad idea?" my twin asks.

"Perhaps both."

"My favorite kind. What is it?"

"Let's go visit our dear sister."

Bash raises the line of his brow. "I have to disagree with you, brother. That is mostly just a bad idea. But I like it just the same."

We walk to the palace, sweat still running down our backs, soaking our t-shirts. Maybe if we wanted to break the rules and show our faces in the fae palace once again, we should have put in more effort and better preparation and dressed accordingly.

But I suppose we are who we are, regardless of how we dress, and if the grass remembers, the palace will too.

By the time we reach the end of the footpath, the sun has risen and the sky is tinged in bright shades of yellow and orange and pink. A flock of birds flies in a V beyond the palace and I immediately ache for my wings.

It's been far too long since I took to the air.

"You think we'll be shot on sight?" Bash asks beside me. There's levity to his voice, but I know he's serious. We very well could be.

The path spills out at the top of a grassy knoll and the palace comes into view.

Bash and I are silent as we take in the sight of it.

It was made of white stone quarried from far underground by an army of brownies. It was constructed into the hillside, so half of it is above ground and the other below. There are numerous spires that twist up toward the sky like the shell of a ladder horn snail.

In the early morning light, the stone glitters.

The sight of our royal home makes my eyes ache.

"This..." Bash clears his throat. "I wasn't prepared to see it," he finishes.

"Neither was I," I admit.

"We could turn back now," he says, his gaze still on the palace. "No one would know."

"We would."

"Suppose we would." He starts forward. "Then when we walk in there, let us walk with our heads held high. We are the fae princes, after all. Banished or not."

We are not shot upon arrival.

"Small victories, eh?" Bash says and waggles his eyebrows at me.

"Not getting shot in the ass. That's the win we're celebrating?"

He laughs as we come up on the gate. There are two guards there, battle swords strapped to their backs.

They look soft around the middle though and bored beyond measure.

That is, until they notice us.

"Your Royal Highnesses," the taller one says and gives us a deep bow. "What a pleasure."

"We'd like to see our sister," Bash says. "Would you be so kind as to let us in?"

The guards share a look.

"If you need to ask permission to conduct your duties," I say, "then go on. We don't have all day."

They mutter and mumble and stumble over themselves. "Of course not, sir. Let us get this open for you." They unlatch the gate and the lever clangs loudly. Each man takes a side and has to manhandle it to swing it open. If I remember correctly, the gate was made by the brownie we killed, the very same that had plotted against Peter Pan.

An excellent craftsman, apparently, but shit at plotting revenge.

Inside the gate, we follow the cobblestone path to the arched double doors that will lead down to the receiving room, and beyond that and underground, the throne room.

When we shove the doors in, they groan loudly on ancient iron hinges. The halls are full of life just as I remember it. Fae with wings and fae with horns and fae with green skin to blend into the vined walls.

They all look at us as we enter, and then look at us again.

Everything is the same and yet everything has changed.

We've yet to be here under our sister's rule. We were banished and removed from the palace within hours of our father's death. Our sister was crowned the next night.

"Who has entered my palace and caused a stir?" Our sister's voice booms through the halls. Bash and I look at one another, slightly impressed.

"It's your handsome older brothers," Bash calls back.

The crowd goes silent.

There are a few more guards here stationed at the entrance to the throne room, but they too look fragile and unprepared. Certainly too distracted by our arrival to be quick on the draw of their swords.

Just what has our sister been doing these last several years? None of her warriors look ready for war.

Bash and I wouldn't have let them get this soft. Never in a million moons.

Tilly comes down off her throne and starts toward us. Her wings are iridescent in the glittering orbs of light that hang from the vined ceiling. She lets them flutter as she nears, as if she's rubbing it in.

Even growing up, our sister was conniving and cruel. She learned from the best, after all. Our mother was the queen of cruelty.

"Leave us," she tells the courtiers and they scatter like flies. The hall and the throne room is empty within moments. I have to admire my sister's hold over them. They may be soft, but at least they obey.

"Get in here," she says, "and shut the door."

As if we follow her commands.

But Bash and I are here on a mission and perhaps it's best to play our parts—for now.

We enter the throne room and shut the inner set of doors with a loud bang. It's a sound that reminds me of my childhood, when Bash and I would sneak into the throne room and hide beneath the tables while our father conducted business. Sometimes he would find us and shoo us away. Sometimes I think he knew we were there and let us stay.

Tilly goes to the bar and fills three goblets with faerie wine. She doesn't serve them to us, though. She leaves them on the bar top. "You're not supposed to be here."

Bash circles the throne room, his hands hanging at his side as if he means no one any harm. "What are you up to, dear sister?"

"Whatever do you mean?"

"Your brownie is dead," I say and take several slow, deliberate steps her way.

She goes rigid and her knuckles turn white as her grip on the glass tightens.

"I wondered where he'd disappeared to," she says, pretending that we haven't just gutted her.

I have to imagine that after she banished us, she was sorely wanting for friends. The brownie was probably the only one she could trust. The fae follow their leaders, until they don't. All it takes is one misstep, one accidental show of weakness, and someone will be challenging our sister to a duel. I'm shocked she hasn't been challenged yet. She's young and inexperienced compared to our past leaders. And she was never meant to rule. Bash and I were to be co-kings. We were born to the throne. She was born to be married off.

"The brownie told us what you were plotting," Bash lies.

Technically, the only thing the brownie told us was that our sister wanted what was best for the island and when we confronted him about our dear sister purposefully scrambling the Darlings' minds, he didn't outright deny it.

Tilly considers us from behind the glare of her wine glass.

Along with being cruel, our sister was also ridiculously competitive growing up. More than once, she beat Bash and me at a game of Bones and Blades. But sometimes, Bash and I let her win just so she wouldn't throw a tantrum.

She has that look on her face now, like she's about to toss the game board across the room.

"You think I don't know what you're doing?" She sips from her glass and then sets it aside. The wine was for us, not her. We'd always had the reputation of being partiers in court. Maybe she was hoping we'd guzzle her wine and get sloppy.

"What are we doing?" Bash asks innocently as he makes his way to the throne and stops at it. Our father had promised us he'd have a second one made so Bash and I could rule side by side. But as the years went on and the second throne failed to appear, Bash and I started to wonder if our father had other plans.

It turned out he did, though it's hard to say how serious he was about it until our mother died. Tink changed everything.

"You're trying to get me to admit something, though what, I don't know. Whatever the brownie told you, it wasn't true," Tilly says. "But if there's something in partic-ular you want, just ask for it."

She takes a few steps to the left, putting equal distance between her and us.

"We want our wings back," I say. "But you already knew that."

"I can't do that. Not when you've been banished."

"We could be unbanished." Kas takes the three steps up the dais and then drapes his arm over the back of the throne and smiles.

I'm not exactly upset that a second throne never appeared, considering this one is ugly beyond reason. It's large and overwhelming and cast of bronze. It has a sunburst as its back, the rays shooting out in shiny bronze. If it had only been that, I might have appreciated it and its simplicity. But whoever designed it must have looked at the sun and said, "More. I need more."

Twining around the sunburst, also in bronze, are vines and squirrels and bees and snakes and frogs and beetles. The feet of the throne are made to look like the paws of a bear, and the curved arms were molded to resemble the talons of a bird.

It's all too much. Just like the fae court. Always too much.

"I can't just rescind your punishment," Tilly says. "Not without a greater reason."

Ahhh, and there it is.

The bait.

Bash and I share a look. We can't use our fae language here to have a secret conversation. Tilly speaks it, after all.

But my twin and I don't always need words to communicate.

"We have nothing to offer you," I say, when really, we have two very big things—two runaway shadows.

Our sister would kill to claim one. I'm sure of it.

She turns to Bash, her long braid sliding over the silky back of her royal blue robe. "You came here for a reason," she says to him. "If it's not to negotiate your return with something I can use, then I fear you're wasting your time."

"The brownie said you wanted Peter Pan dead," Bash says.

She freezes.

That one was also a lie—the brownie told us no such thing—but we know it to be true.

"He killed our mother," Tilly says as if she needs to defend herself. "He lost his shadow. Peter Pan retiring has been needed for a very long time."

"And by retiring you mean..." I let the sentence trail off.

"Dead," Bash fills in.

Tilly somehow manages to look ashamed of this suggestion.

"And if we were to help with this mission," I continue.

"Then you, our dear sister, would..." Kas adds.

"Give you back your wings," she says quietly.

There is nothing I want more than that.

Well...perhaps also my rightful place at the helm of the fae court. Not because I want to rule, but because I was born to do it. And I take duty very seriously. It feels like an itch I cannot scratch.

Bash pivots away from the throne. "And our banishment?"

"I can give you back your wings, but the court would never accept your return—"

"Bullshit," Bash says.

"Do you even know why we killed our father?" I ask.

Bash shoots a look my way. This question is toeing the line of too goddamn personal, but I need her to know. I need her to know why we made the decision we did.

"You were angry at him," she answers, which is about as vague as you can get.

"Of course we were angry at him." Bash plucks one of the spindly twigs from the vines growing in the walls and twists it into a knot.

"But why were we angry?" I ask her and catch the faint dip in her throat as she swallows.

"We were angry," Bash says, "because he told us he planned to disinherit us from the throne."

We both watch for her reaction. Our sister may be cunning, but she could never hide from us.

I'm surprised to see no reaction at all.

Time for the next secret to test her. "Father was dying already, did you know that?"

Her mouth pops open.

Finally, we've managed to surprise her.

"He wanted his revenge against Peter Pan for killing Tink, so he swam into the lagoon hoping it would imbue him with more power. Instead, he came out dying."

"So he scrambled to make a plan," Bash says. "But his plan was never to allow his sons to take over.

"'You sympathize with Peter Pan,' he'd told us. 'You don't deserve to rule.'"

"So he schemed behind our backs," I say. "He wanted

the island to unite against Peter Pan and he knew he was running out of time to do it himself. So he offered *your* hand in marriage to Captain Hook and Hook agreed."

"He was going to auction you off like chattel," Bash says, his voice catching.

"And that is why we killed him," I finish. "To protect you and to protect our rightful place among the court."

Our sister blinks. But her mouth is pursed tightly again and all of the blood leaves my face.

I'm numb all over, but suddenly covered in a cold sweat.

She knew.

She fucking knew?

Bash and I glance at one another and I can see my own rage reflected in his eyes.

After we killed our father, we were immediately isolated from our sister and were never given an opportunity to explain. We blamed it on the other noble fae who never quite liked us, who had always wanted a puppet on the throne.

It made sense to us.

But maybe it was Tilly all along.

I'm going to kill her, I tell my brother.

I'll help you, he says.

We charge for her.

"Stop!" she yells and throws out her hand and the floor beneath our feet turns to quicksand.

I stagger. Bash hits his knees and his hands get stuck in the mire.

It's all an illusion. I know this magic. I can even smell the faintness of it on the air. Sweet like honeysuckle, edged in earthiness like that of sweetgrass.

I'm surprised that I'm having a very difficult time fighting it.

Our dear sister has become more powerful in our absence.

Tilly takes in a long, settling breath.

"Yes, I knew what our father planned to do." She clasps her hands behind her back, her iridescent eyes glittering. "He came to me first because he knew I would do what needed to be done. Neither of you were ever driven enough to make the sacrifices the fae needed. Peter Pan killed our mother and you barely blinked."

"Did he not have a right to his revenge?" Bash bites out. "Mother was a cold-hearted bitch who betrayed him. Say what you will about Pan—he may be cruel and he may be vicious, but you will never wake up with his knife in your back."

Tilly's wings flutter angrily behind her and the edges turn bright crimson. "Father was right to disinherit you. You dishonor the fae. I don't regret the decisions I made. I would have married Captain Hook and we would have banded together to defeat Peter Pan."

"And then what? The fae queen would have a pirate for a husband?"

"Was our mother not a common fae? And she made her place among the court just like Hook would have."

I snort. "I don't buy that for a second."

She screws up her mouth. "All right, yes. He would have been a thorn in my side. The men of Neverland have always felt they deserved to rule, even when they don't."

She turns again, her wings going still. "I would have done then what I plan to do now."

"Which is what?"

The smile that comes to her full lips is devilish indeed. "Summon his greatest fear to deal with him, so I can rule all of Neverland alone."

She's so smug and proud about it, our dear little sister. How much she's changed beneath the cutthroat world of the fae court.

"I know I can do better," she adds. "I *will* do better."

I hear the words she's left unsaid. "Tilly, what have you done?" I yank at the quicksand but it holds fast and sucks me deeper.

"Two birds, one stone. Remember that saying? It used to be Nani's favorite."

"Spit it out, dear sister," Bash says and lunges forward, testing the sand's strength.

"There is one man who can handle both Hook and Peter Pan."

I go cold inside.

"No," Bash says. "Don't tell me—"

"The Crocodile," she says.

"Fuck."

Tilly smiles. "Getting inside of the Darlings' heads all of those years has allowed me to reap something of value— Peter Pan's secrets. He has been keeping something from the Crocodile and he won't be happy when he finds out. When all is said and done, the Crocodile will have devoured both Pan and Hook and I will be the only one left standing."

She turns away, her wings closing at her back. The floor returns to stone and we are immediately free.

"I suggest you pick a side," she says as she walks away. "And if you want to live, I suggest you pick mine."

16

WINNIE

I wake to the hard press of Peter Pan's cock at the small of my back.

The room is dark and quiet and it's impossible to tell what time it is. I feel muzzy with sleep, but rested, and I suspect that must have something to do with all of the fucking and the excitement and the hot water of the bath and Peter Pan curling his body against mine as we went to bed.

My heart is content and happy and I'm terrified that it will all end soon.

How do I hold on to this?

How do I make it mine?

I don't want to break this bubble and be forced to return home to a life that never fit and one I never wanted.

If I just hold on...hold on...

I stretch, rousing Pan, and he pushes his hips toward me, rubbing his cock against me.

He inhales and nuzzles his nose into the back of my

neck, tightening his hold around my waist.

Pan said he's unsure of where he came from, but sometimes I wonder if he's an ancient god because I want to worship him.

Every second I'm with him feels like a goddamn miracle.

"Are you awake, Darling?" he asks, his voice thick with sleep.

"Sorta."

He stretches with me, tangling his legs with mine. "How did you sleep?"

"Better than I have in a long time. Every night on Neverland is better than the last."

On another inhale, he drinks in my scent and then places a warm kiss on my bare shoulder and then—

He grumbles a little in the back of his throat.

"What is it?" I ask.

"Vane is coming," he says.

Cold shoulder. Cold shoulder, I remind myself, even though my entire body is singing and my insides coil up like a spring.

"Tell him to go away," I say.

"You try telling the Dark One to go away and see what you get." He chuckles and drags me closer. "He'll come around one day, Darling," he assures me. "I think when this is all over, he'll return to his island and give up his shadow."

I spin toward him. "He'll what?"

The tomb door clanks open and murky light filters in. Vane reaches for the light switch and the lamp comes on and I clamp my hand over my eyes as the burn of the light assaults me.

"Why am I not surprised to find a whore in your bed,"

Vane says.

I pull my hand away and try to scowl over at him, but it's impossible when he looks the way he does.

He's in a black button-up shirt that for some damn reason is mostly unbuttoned and tucked into black trousers. The metal clasp of a belt flares above his groin and I'm parched, just thinking about undoing it and seeing what he has to offer.

There is a cigarette dangling from his mouth, the smoke curling around his face. The light of the stairwell behind him paints him in strokes of gold.

But it's the black eye and the violet one pinned on me that does me in.

I swallow loudly. I know he notices.

I try to meet his insult with something clever but all I get out is, "Better a whore than none at all."

"You could join us," Pan says behind me and I stiffen in his grip.

My neck is still aching from last night, the terror still fresh. I both want and don't want Vane to give in. It's like deciding to jump out of a plane. You know it'll be an adventure to talk about for years, but at the same time, what if your parachute fails? You won't be telling anyone about it because you'll be fucking dead.

"You know me, Pan," Vane says as he leans a shoulder against the open doorway. "I don't waste my time with easy pussy."

I bristle. Motherfucking fuck—

I slide from the bed completely naked. Vane's gaze dips to my tits, then down to the V between my legs before racing back up to meet my eyes as if suddenly remembering he hates me.

"If you hate easy pussy, then why fuck Cherry?"

Not missing a beat, he says, "Because she's not you."

That stings more than I want it to and I know it registers on my face like a slap.

For the briefest of seconds, I swear Vane's expression falls as if he wants to take back his words.

But then I remind myself of Pan's advice. I'm clearly trying too hard. I need to try less.

"Fair enough," I say. "I should go up and see if the twins have made coffee." I put a knee to the bed's edge, purposefully giving Vane my ass as I bend over to kiss Pan on the lips. I linger there, arching my back, pushing my ass out, spreading my legs a little so Vane can see all of me.

Pan smiles at me, knowing what I'm doing. "Careful, Darling," he purrs.

"Of course, my king. I'll be a good girl. Just for you."

I hear Vane grumble behind me.

Pan kisses me again, long and deep, his tongue meeting mine.

I'm immediately wet. But it's not just because of the kiss. It's because of Vane watching us.

Why hasn't he come over? When will he give in?

And was Pan serious when he said Vane was going to return to his island to give his shadow back? Why does that make me feel full of ice and nettles?

When Pan breaks the kiss, I'm a little dizzy and when I right myself with two feet on the floor, I sway.

Vane is suddenly there catching me. His teeth clench, jaw flexing and then his gaze goes to my neck where I'm sure the skin is still bruised from his touch.

"Tell the twins to put some salve on that," he orders me. "It'll help with the bruising."

Why can I not take a full breath?

My heart is a rapid thump in my ears. Vane's hands are

still on me and he's so close I can feel the heat of his breath on my skin. I'm covered in goosebumps and tighter than a spring.

How can I give him the cold shoulder when he acts like this?

I am a flower trapped in a slant of shade, desperate for his light.

And maybe that's the cruelest part of all of this. The fact that he can be that way with me and then hate me immediately after.

"Go on," he says. "I need to speak to the king."

I gulp down a breath and give him a quick nod before retrieving my clothing and hurrying up the stairs.

I find the twins in the kitchen and both seem in a mood.

They're both shirtless. Bash's hair is wet like he just took a shower. It shines like a slick of oil in the light. He's at the island mixing together ingredients while Kas leans against the counter behind him, a cup of coffee in hand.

It's already dark beyond the windows and I can barely make out the stretch of the ocean.

I guess when you're entangled with a king who can't see sunlight, there is no such thing as day anymore.

"Hi," I say.

The twins barely notice me.

Bash upends a cup of flour over a bowl and then stirs it roughly, causing the flour to cloud into the air.

"Everything all right?" I ask.

Kas blinks back to reality and turns toward me. He smiles, but his mouth is tight across his bright white teeth. "Everything is fine."

I reach past him for the French press and pour myself a cup of coffee.

They seem tense.

I'm tense too after that run-in with Vane and I automatically want to liven the mood and make myself feel better.

I set the coffee down and step in front of Kas. He looks down the sharp slant of his nose at me. "Are you sure you're all right?" I ask and cup his balls through his shorts.

He lets out a low groan.

Bash's stirring stalls behind me.

"We have a lot on our mind, Darling," Kas says.

"Like what?"

The sound of tinkling bells fills the air. I know now that the sound means the twins are talking to one another in their fae language and purposefully leaving me out.

I stroke Kas, feel him start to engorge beneath my hand. His teeth grit when he looks away from his brother and back at me. "You really don't want to do this right now, Darling."

"Oh, really?"

"Darling," Bash says behind me. "We've had a rather complicated day."

Why is everyone suddenly turning me away?

I huff out a breath and go to Bash and shove my hand down his pants. He jolts, growls, and sets the mixing bowl aside. "Fine," I say and fist him tightly. "I guess I'll just have to go occupy myself."

His gaze burns into me as I stroke him, his teeth gritting as I turn him hard in an instant.

"Carry on." I smile sweetly up at him and then walk away, the sound of tinkling bells following me out of the room.

17

ARE WE GOING TO LET HER GET AWAY WITH THAT? I ASK MY brother.

We're watching the Darling walk away, smugly satisfied with herself, leaving us both fucking hard and wanting.

After our sister let us walk right out of the fae palace, my brother and I have been stewing over her threats.

There is no easy route to any of this and it's really pissing me off.

Who do we owe the most allegiance to?

Peter Pan would never betray us. But he might kill us if we step out of line.

Our sister would betray us just as easily as she would the stableboy, but kill us? I'm not so sure. I think we could do a great many horrible things and our sister would never raise a hand to us.

Which is worse?

I don't want to ask the question and I certainly don't want to fucking answer it.

I want to forget about all of it.

I catch sight of the Darling's ass as she rounds the corner. She's always wearing those fucking dresses, her pussy always so closely within reach, her tits bouncing beneath the soft material, her nipples peaked, begging for teeth and tongue.

It takes no effort at all to conjure an image of her hands tied behind her back and the image builds pressure in my head until I can think of nothing else other than to fuck.

I can't tell if my desire to pound some sense into her is a good or bad thing, Kas says.

Why can't it be both? I reply.

We look at one another.

Get the rope, Kas says.

You don't have to tell me twice.

Kas runs to head her off and I fetch the rope from our room.

When I return to the loft, my dear brother has Darling pressed to the trunk of the Never Tree. She's trembling beneath him, occupied by his lips. So when I snatch her wrist and double loop the rope around her, it catches her off guard.

A cute little breath hiccups past her lips.

I am an experienced knotter and I have both arms tied to the tree in less than thirty seconds.

Kas and I step back to admire my handy work. I've used a single column tie on both her wrists and lashed her to low hanging branches of the Never Tree. They are good, basic knots. Easy to undo. Hard to get out of.

"Look at our Darling," I tell my brother. "Trussed up like the naughty little girl she is."

She struggles against the ropes. She won't get out. Not unless I want her to.

She rises on her tiptoes, her dress creeping up her thighs.

I go to her. She's tiny next to me and her smallness makes my gut clench. "What did you think would happen, Darling? You don't get to touch our cocks and then skip away."

Blood is pooling in the apples of her cheeks. "Maybe this is where I wanted to end up all along."

I laugh. I actually believe her. I'm going to make her regret it.

She stops fighting the ropes. "Well, you have me held captive, fae prince. Now what do you plan to do with me?"

"What do you think, brother?" I say over my shoulder.

Kas comes up beside me, his arms crossed over his chest. "I say we prolong the lesson."

"Mmmm. And what did you have in mind?"

There is a dark, devious fire burning in the center of my chest. I want to see the Darling beg for it. I want her to moan and writhe and lose her fucking mind the way I do every time she walks in the fucking room.

I want her to distract me from my own aching heart.

"She wants to throw her body at us," Kas says, watching the Darling's face turn redder by the second. "So let's make her come so much it hurts."

My cock strains against my pants. I am impatient to be inside of her. But the sooner I take that pussy, the sooner I'll come.

"I like it." I step into her and trail a finger down her cheek. She exhales in an excited gasp. "How many times do you think we can make her come? Three? Five? Ten?"

"There's only one way to find out," Kas says. "Are you ready, Darling? When we're done with you, you'll be begging us to stop."

18

Strung up in the Never Tree, I can't help but feel like a bug that accidentally flew too close to a spiderweb.

Kas knows what he's doing when it comes to tying ropes and no amount of struggling or yanking or wiggling is helping.

I'm not going anywhere any time soon and the fae princes know it.

They circle me and my clit tingles with anticipation.

They're going to make this oh-so worth it.

"What do you think, brother?" Bash says as he disappears from my line of sight. "Should we give her a safe word?"

Kas drags the point of his knuckle down my cheek. "She comes once for us, then she gets to pick whatever word she wants."

He bends down and plants a gentle kiss at the corner of my mouth. I turn to him, trying to capture his lips, but he's already pulled away.

Bash's hands come to the hem of my dress and yank it up. He clucks his tongue. "I don't think you should be allowed to wear panties anymore."

"I would agree," Kas says and relieves me of them in one quick yank.

"Maybe she shouldn't be allowed to wear any clothes at all." Bash lets the skirt of my dress drop back down, then slides his hand up the curve of my waist to my breast. His touch is patient as he presses into my ass, letting me know he's hard for me.

"I can't just walk around naked," I say.

"Why not?" he purrs against my ear. "Then we could admire you at all hours of the day and night. Have you dripping wet whenever we'd like, with nothing to stand between us." He rubs at my nipple, coaxing it to bead.

Kas's hand trails up my thigh and stops dangerously close to the hollow between my legs.

I breathe out quickly in anticipation.

"How fast can we make her come?" Bash says.

Kas smirks and teases at my clit with his clever fingers and I sink against the ropes, desperate for more of him. "Minutes, if that."

"You want the honor?" Bash asks.

"I will gladly take it."

Kas covers my mound with his large hand. The sensation sends heat pooling to my clit and I instinctively rub against him. "That's my girl," Kas says, low and guttural. He spreads his fingers over me, wiggles them, and pressure builds in my clit as Bash reaches around from me behind me to pinch at my nipple.

I mewl for them.

Kas slips a finger inside of me and puts pressure on my clit with the heel of his hand.

"Make yourself come," he orders.

"W-what?"

"Grind against me," he says. "And make yourself come. Do it now, Darling."

When Kas commands me, I want to comply. I want to please him. Because he commands so infrequently, every command feels weightier.

It takes me a second to find my footing and balance, but once I do and circle my hips, I find the right amount of friction on his hand. He helps me too, following my rhythm by pressing the heel of his hand in just the right way, at just the right time.

"You hear how wet she is, brother?" Kas says.

"Fuck yeah, I do." Bash's left hand drifts up to my throat, while his other hand squeezes my breast and plays with my nipple.

It doesn't take me long to reach the precipice.

I grind hard against Bash's hand as Kas's grip on my throat tightens.

"She's growing wetter by the second," Kas says.

I'm panting hard now, driving quickly against Kas and so fucking close. "Go on, Darling," Kas says. "Take what you've earned like a good little whore."

He adds his thick middle finger to my opening and fills me up, rubbing the palm of his hand against me as my movements grow frenzied and my breathing quicker.

"Fuck, Darling," Bash says at my ear. "I can't wait to fill you up too. I'm going to take your ass, stretch you around my cock."

I moan out in surprise and his grip on my throat tightens. "Then my brother will take your pussy—"

"Finally," Kas says.

"And you'll be full of fae cock."

"But first," Kas nips at my bottom lip. "First, you need to come for us."

I rock against his palm. Bash pinches my nipple between two fingers, causing me to yelp in pain.

And Kas hits my clit just right, forcing the orgasm out of me.

I slam down on his hand and he shoves up inside of me. Kas holds me fast against his chest as the ropes creak and the bindings on my wrist bite against my flesh.

The orgasm pounds through every hollow, burning through every nerve as my own pleasure drenches me and Kas.

"Fuck yeah," Kas says. "Fuck, she's clenching so tight around me."

"Our little Darling likes being used." Bash angles me to the side, his mouth coming to my ear. "You hear that, Darling?"

Kas drags his fingers out of me, then shoves back in, making a loud wet noise. "That's the sound of your defeat."

They leave me tied up but step back to admire me. My legs are weak, but I'm still glowing brightly from the orgasm. Fuck if I don't love when the twins turn devious.

When not fucking or playing with me, they're jovial and kind, but they are experts at being wicked and depraved.

"What shall her safe word be?" Bash crosses the room and goes to what remains of the bar. There are just three bottles left. He twists off the cap and pulls out two glasses and fills each with a few fingers of spiced rum.

"Do you have a preference, Darling?" Kas asks. He's leaning against the back of one of the leather chairs, his arms crossed over his chest. Several dark tendrils of hair have fallen out of his bun, making him look disheveled and wild. Every cut of muscle seems extra taut today, like he's tense or hasn't eaten enough in the last twenty-four hours.

Something is definitely bothering them, but I seem to be reaping the benefit of it.

The air around them practically—

"Crackle," I blurt.

Bash hands Kas a glass of rum and comes to stand beside him. "Crackle? All right."

"Crackle it is." Kas takes a long pull from the glass, draining half of it and then comes over to me. "Drink." He brings the glass to my lips and tips it slowly. The alcohol fills my mouth with its smooth sweetness and then burns down my throat as I swallow it.

"You ready to come again?" he asks me, his amber eyes sparking with hunger.

"I don't think I can."

"Do you doubt me?"

I inhale, taking in the scent of him. He reminds me of being on the beach on a cool, rainy summer night. The smell of the sand, the salty air, the headiness of the darkness and the crashing of waves. The salty spray hitting your skin.

I haven't known him long, but I think he is a man I could fall in love with quickly.

Kas slides his hand along my jawline and brings my face up to him. "Darling? Do you doubt me?" he repeats, just as something soft slithers up my legs. I look down to see a vine twining around my calves.

A sharp gasp rushes down my throat and Kas forces my face up again, forcing me to look at him as the vine slithers up to my pussy.

I don't know if this is actually happening or if it's one of his clever illusions, but it feels very, very real as a soft, feathered tendril flicks at my pussy.

Oh god.

I'm pulsing again, needy for more.

"No," I say on a pant. "I don't doubt you."

"Good." And then he steps back to join his brother as the vines slither over my body. A thick tendril slides up the wet center of me and twines around my waist so every tiny movement sends a tingling sensation to my core.

More vines steal beneath my dress, to tease at my nipples and squeeze at my breasts.

I'm panting and buzzing within seconds as the twins stand by and watch.

"Oh fuck." I moan loudly when a cool, nubby vine slithers inside of me. "Oh my god."

Every nerve in my body is burning brightly.

My knees turn weak and I slump in the ropes.

The vine fucks me harder and several feathered tendrils caress my buzzing clit. There are so many. I'm on sensory overload and I couldn't stop the orgasm if I tried.

I hang my head back, eyes slammed closed as the orgasm slams through me.

The ropes groan. The Never Tree shakes as I fight for tension and control.

When I slip down the other side of the pleasure, I can barely stand and I'm shaking so badly, my teeth chatter.

Kas comes over. "No," I say. "Please. I can't do anymore."

His eyes burn brightly. "Yes, you can."

Bash drains his glass in one gulp and sets it down with a loud clang.

"I can't." I'm drenched from my own juices and my clit is buzzing like a live wire. "No more."

"Loosen the ropes," Bash says. "Let's make her sit on my face."

"What? No. No, no." Oh shit. Do I use my safe word? Do I want to? I like toeing the line with them. I like pushing the boundaries. I like feeling the edge of pain with the caress of pleasure.

But I seriously don't know how much more I can take.

I've never been with men like the twins, who are not only relentless, but damn near diabolical with pleasure.

I never in a million years thought I'd be begging not to orgasm.

Together, the twins loosen the ropes tied to the tree and I'm so weak, I automatically sink to the floor to my knees. Once I'm in the position they want me, they refasten the ropes.

Kas steps back again as Bash sits on the floor in front of me, his back to me. All of the deliberate lines of his tattoos stand out against his skin. He grins at me over his shoulder. "Lift up, Darling."

Reluctantly, I find the last bit of strength in my legs and rise up enough so that Bash can lie back and settle in between my legs. He takes in a deep breath. "Fuck, you smell so sweet, Darling."

The ropes creak again as my thighs quiver and I resettle right over his mouth.

I can feel the heat of his breath on my wet pussy. He folds up the skirt of my dress and bunches it around my waist, baring me, and then hooks his arms over my thighs where my legs meet my hips.

"So my brother can watch," Bash says, and then he devours me.

19

DARLING STRUGGLES AGAINST THE ROPES. SHE'S SQUIRMING AS MY brother takes her in his mouth. Watching the pleasure and the pain dance across her face is a sight I want to burn to memory.

God, she is a vision.

I don't want to let her go.

I can't let her go.

She is a quicksand I will welcome. We will never get out and I don't want to.

Pull me under, Darling.

When she comes a third time, I can tell it edges on painful. She must be burning up, her clit so sensitive it hurts.

But we always stick to our word, my brother and I.

We do what we say we'll do.

Forcing the Darling to come again and again is a gift I didn't know I needed.

When Bash slides out from beneath her, he's covered in

her juices and he cleans them off with a swipe of his tongue.

Darling is breathing hard, covered in sweat.

I'm hard as stone, ready to fuck and take.

She'll have the choice to stop us, but I hope she doesn't.

She barely notices when we refasten the ropes, bring her to her feet. Her eyes are heavy, her body boneless. When I come around to face her, her lashes flutter against her cheeks.

"Darling," I say and tip her chin up. Her eyes pop open. "Are you still with us?"

She nods emphatically. "I'm here."

"One more," I tell her.

"No," she says on a moan.

"Yes."

Her tongue darts out, wetting her parched lips. She has her safe word, but her mouth won't form it and a depraved part of me is terrified she will.

Don't say it, Darling.

Keep it tucked behind your teeth.

Bash spits on his hand and grips his dick. Darling's pussy is soaked for me. I won't need any help.

Ready? Bash asks.

Fuck yes.

Bash winds his arm around her waist and I take her thighs and wrap her legs around me, lining myself up.

I've yet to have her pussy. There is nothing I've ever wanted more.

Bash guides himself into her ass and she moans loudly, eyes squeezed shut. I don't know if she's been fucked in the ass, but there will be plenty more of it after today.

I let him settle into her first. Because when I finally get inside her pussy, I will not be gentle.

"How's she feel?" I ask him.

"Fucking tight, brother. *Fucking tight.*" His eyes roll back as he lifts her up and off his cock, and then slides slowly back in.

"Darling?" I say and her eyes flutter open again. Sometimes when we use illusion magic, a mortal can get lost to the feel of it and I need to know she's still here. "One more," I tell her.

She nods as my twin fills her up again. "Fuck me, Kas," she says. "I want you to come inside of me."

I will not deny my Darling girl.

And as I slam into her, as she clenches around me as we fuck her together, hard and fast and relentless, I realize one terrifying truth—I will pick her over Tilly and the fae court.

I will pick Darling over my own wings because with her I am already flying.

She is mine and I am hers.

20

WINNIE

THE TWINS FUCK ME SO HARD, MY TEETH CLACK TOGETHER. IF IT wasn't for the ropes, I think I might be launched to the rafters.

The vines return, teasing at my clit as the brothers fill me with fae cock.

"We come together," Kas says on heated breaths. "You hear me, Darling?"

My clit is so sensitive, it hurts. But I nod because I can't deny him. I won't.

The build of pleasure this time is a slow crawl, and it's clear the brothers mean to wrench the orgasm from me if it's the last thing they do.

"Come for us, Darling," Bash says at my ear, his voice ragged and hoarse. "One last time."

"Oh god." I choke down a breath, trying to fill my lungs with oxygen. "Fuck. *Yes*." When I reach the crest of the wave, there is a moment of nothingness. Time seems to slow. I am a bird with her wings open, caught in a head-wind. And then...and then...

"Fuck! Oh fuck, oh god!" I'm sailing, crashing. I don't know up from down. There is only the overwhelming wave of pleasure and pain and I sink into it, revel in it, let it consume me as the brothers pound into my pussy and my ass.

"Oh fuck, Darling," Kas says and slams into me, unloading into me and Bash tightens his grip on me, filling up my ass with his cum.

We stay locked together for what feels like forever, sticky and sweaty and spent.

Bash breathes hard into my ear and Kas sinks into me, resting his forehead against mine as his cock throbs out the last of his pleasure.

And then he kisses me long and deep, and when he pulls back, he says, "You are a wonder, Darling. And you are ours."

I nod because it's true and I want it to always be true.

When they finally pull out of me and step back, I notice they both look past me and the Never Tree to where the stairs spill into the loft.

Heavy footsteps come over and Peter Pan comes into my line of sight. I can only imagine how I must look. Messy and used. Like a good little whore and I brighten beneath his bright blue stare.

"Word of advice, Darling," Pan says, "never let the twins tie you up."

I summon the last bit of energy I have and smile sweetly up at him. "I don't know. I rather enjoyed it."

Vane yanks open one of the knots and the rope drops from the branch of the Never Tree and Pan catches me as I sag. When the second rope is undone, Vane comes over and unties my wrists. "I told you to ask them for salve," he says, his voice edged in annoyance, "not another brutal fucking."

"I do what I want," I tell him with a laugh that edges on madness.

He scowls at me, but his fingers are gentle as he undoes the knots. "Get the salve," he tells them.

As soon as I'm untied, Pan scoops me into his arms and carries me over to his chair. He sits down, tucks me into the crook of his arm. "Get her a drink," he tells Vane and for some reason the Dark One doesn't balk.

He returns a few seconds later with a fresh glass of bourbon and holds it to my lips. "Drink," he orders.

If I had known getting fucked hard by the twins would make Vane take care of me, I would have done it a lot sooner.

I drink and the buzzy warmth of the alcohol soothes some of the knots in my flesh.

It's Kas that returns with this mysterious fairy salve in a circular metal jar. He twists off the lid to reveal a green goo that glitters in the light.

He takes my left arm in hand, then dips two fingers into the goo with his other. When he rubs the salve into the tender flesh of my wrist, I hiss out in pain, but he holds me fast and within seconds, the goo turns warm and comforting, sending a tingling sensation down my arm.

"Better?" Kas asks.

I nod and collapse back against Pan, resting my head on his shoulder. "That feels good."

"You assholes shouldn't have gone so hard on her," Vane says.

Pan's voice rumbles behind me. "You nearly killed her last night, so you can shut your fucking mouth." He points at the twins. "And you two assholes need to ease her into your fucked up twin shit."

"Oh, excuse me, Never King," Bash says. "'*Crawl to me, Darling.*' You like our little Darling submissive but only when it serves you and—"

"Stop!" I say.

They all go quiet. Pan tenses beneath me. "Let's get something straight." With the fairy salve soaking into my bloodstream, I feel loads better and I lift my head off Pan's shoulder to look at all of them. "You're all assholes, all right? But you're *my* assholes. I didn't have to stay on my knees for Pan and I didn't have to push Vane to the brink and I certainly didn't have to get tied to a tree.

"I chose those things. I choose all of you. Even you, Vane. So stop treating me like a fragile toy. I'm not. I'm a china cup that has been broken so many times that I'm never sure if I'm a cup or just separate pieces held together by glue and sheer determination, molded into a cup-like shape. I know how to crack and I know how to mend. At least with you all, I know I will never mend alone."

They look between one another.

"Suppose she's right," Bash says. "The Darling knows what she wants. She always has." He winks at me. He was the first to fuck me, after all. The first to break rank. And I'm grateful to him for it. If he hadn't, I'm not sure Pan would have given in, or Kas.

Even Vane.

Vane drops into one of the chairs and puts a cigarette into his mouth, and lights the end with a lighter. After he's inhaled and exhaled, he nods at Kas. "Don't forget her neck."

Pan tilts my chin up, exposing the column of my throat

to Kas, but I bat his hand away and look squarely at Vane. "These marks I'll keep, thank you."

He scowls at me, the cigarette burning like a wick from between his fingers.

Once my wrists are done, Kas caps the tin and drops onto the sofa next to his brother. They share a cigarette, passing it back and forth. I'm coming to realize they share everything, including me.

"Let's discuss the plan," Pan says and readjusts me in his lap so I'm cradled against his chest, his hand resting on my shoulder. "Vane got us permission to enter Hook's territory tomorrow night."

"At the expense of what?" Bash asks.

"Cherry."

Kas hands the cigarette back to his brother. "Does she know that?"

"Of course she does," Vane answers.

"And how'd she take it?" Bask asks.

Vane takes another hit from his cigarette and holds the smoke in his lungs and says nothing. Bash laughs. "That well, huh?"

I sink into the warmth of Pan as he fingers the ends of my hair and sends goosebumps running down my arms. "Does she not want to go back?"

"We told her she was free to go home years ago," Bash says. "And she chose to stay."

"She wants the Dark One," Kas says. "Going back to her brother's territory means she will have significantly less opportunity to have him."

"She's not getting me anyway." Vane stabs the cigarette into a glass ashtray on the coffee table and the embers spit out in an arch. "So I don't know why the fuck it matters."

"Where is she?" I ask. I've barely seen her since we came back to Neverland.

I wanted to befriend her, but I think she might slowly come to hate me. Especially if I get my way. *I* want Vane. He *will* give in to me. Eventually.

Maybe Cherry returning to the pirates' end of the island is a good thing.

"I haven't seen her since we returned," Vane answers and runs his hand through his dark hair. "She was in a pissy mood."

"Should I talk to her?" I ask.

Vane cuts his gaze to me. "What would be the point? She's going back home. That's the end of it."

"There's something else we should discuss," Bash says.

Kas spreads his long arms over the back of the couch. "Something neither of you will like."

"Well, don't leave me in suspense," Pan says.

"We visited our dear sister," Kas answers.

I feel the hard line of Pan beneath me grow harder still. "And?"

"And she is plotting against you," Bash adds.

Vane gets up to fetch the bourbon and one of the parakeets flaps away from the bar seeing him advance. It comes to rest on the arm of Pan's chair and chirps sweetly up at me. I try not to make any sudden movements for fear of scaring it away.

It has the softest looking feathers on its breast the color of sunrise, with a run of yellow down its head.

Pan curls a lock of my hair around his index finger. "What aren't you saying, fae princes? Are you planning to turn on me too?"

"If we were," Bash says, "we wouldn't be here, now, would we?"

"Tilly has called someone back to the island," Kas explains. "Someone she thinks will help her stage this coup. Against Pan and Hook."

Pan looks over his shoulder at Vane. They share an unspoken conversation.

I get the distinct sense everyone knows something I don't.

"What is it?" I ask. "Tell me. Who is this enemy?"

Vane puts his hands on the edge of the bar top and hunches over, bowing his head.

The bird chirps and flaps away.

"Tell me," I coax.

"It's Vane's brother," Kas says. "The Crocodile."

21

DARLING SITS FORWARD ON MY LAP AND ROCKS HER ASS AGAINST my cock. I have to bury a groan and try to focus on anything other than every single part of her body.

I'm not sure I'll get anything done if she really does stay. I will always be chasing her pussy and the way she makes me feel when I'm buried inside of her.

But there's no time for that.

Not when the Crocodile is on his way to Neverland.

I wanted to control the Crocodile's presence on the island. I've clearly been too late in that.

"Okay, wait," Darling says, "Hook and Pan share an enemy and it's Vane's brother? And he's...a crocodile?"

Her confusion is adorable.

I suppose in a place like Neverland, compared to her mortal world, Vane having a brother that's a reptile isn't so far-fetched.

"First of all," I correct, and grab her by the arms and tug her back into me if only to feel her closeness. "He isn't my enemy. Not exactly. And second of all, he's a man. His nick-name is The Crocodile."

"Because he eats men like us for breakfast," Bash answers. "I am a tasty snack, after all."

Leave it to Bash to make jokes in a time like this.

"He isn't your enemy yet," Vane points out. "But he will be. And what do you want to bet the Fae Queen knows how to make him one?"

Bash tips his finger at Vane. "You hit the nail on the head. She was dangling secrets in front of us."

My chest tightens, thinking of Tilly knowing any of my business secrets. But of course she does—she's been digging inside the heads of Darlings for centuries. And now she's going to use the information against me.

Darling leaves my lap to pace the living room and I immediately miss her warmth. I want to yank her back down, keep her caged to my chest. When will I get to enjoy her? First my shadow, then Tilly, now Vane's brother.

War is about to break out on Neverland.

I need my fucking shadow. I need the power rushing through my veins.

No one will be able to stand in my way if I am whole again. The island and I will be one and the same and there will be no one greater.

"Okay, hold on," Darling says as she whirls around. "Vane has a brother?" she repeats like the news hasn't quite settled in.

Vane hands me a drink. "We're nothing alike."

Kas snorts. "They are exactly alike. But Roc is taller."

"And better looking," Bash adds.

Vane rolls his eyes and drops back into his chair. "The facts are, Darling, that my dear brother will have a bone to pick with our infamous Never King when he finds out the secrets he's been keeping."

I shoot Vane a look that could melt the meat from his bones. Fucker.

"What secrets?" Darling asks.

When I told Vane I felt no remorse about what I'd done to Wendy, I was telling the truth. But, now faced with sharing the same admission with Darling, I'm overcome with guilt.

I don't ever ask for forgiveness, but I can feel the shape of the begging on the tip of my tongue already.

Fucking hell.

I meet her inquiring gaze. "I've always brought the Darlings back," I say, "all but one."

She cocks her head. "What do you mean?"

"Your great-great grandmother Wendy," I say.

The suspicion bleeds into her face one flinch at a time. "No," she says.

"Yes."

"How...*where*?"

"He took a wrong turn on the way back," Vane says. "And left her on an island known as Everland."

Color paints Darling's cheeks a pretty shade of angry red. "Tell me that's not true."

"I can't. I won't."

"*Pan*!"

I sigh and scratch at the back of my head. "It was a very long time ago, Darling, and I was a much different man."

"You left her?!"

"Looks like you're sleeping on the couch tonight," Bash says.

"Careful, prince. I'm not above paying Vane to fly you to the sky and then drop you through the clouds."

"You have to go get her!" Darling's voice is rising higher and higher by the second. "Right now!"

"Wendy Darling is not my problem." I get to my feet, annoyed that she's standing over me telling me what to do. Pretty Darling girls do not give me orders. "And her being off Neverland is much better for us when the Crocodile arrives anyway."

She crosses her arms over her chest. "How do you figure?"

"Because I will use the information as leverage and once he finds out where she is, he'll be eager to race off to fetch her."

"Why?"

I steal a glance at Vane, trying to gauge how he feels about all of this. Sometimes I wonder if he hates the Darlings so much because of his brother's history with one.

"Because the Crocodile was in love with Wendy."

"Until she tore out his heart," Vane says.

Darling clamps her mouth shut.

Vane drains the last of his liquor and leaves.

"Vane, wait," I try, but he's already gone, already thudding down the stairs.

"Did she...literally tear out his heart?" Darling asks, grimacing.

Kas laughs. "No. *Figuratively,* this time."

"So my great-great grandmother was in love with Vane's brother?"

"Hard to say if her feelings were genuine," Bash says. "She was a tricky minx just like you. You'd love her, you know."

Earnest desire flashes in her eyes. I think Darling has been craving family for a very long time and now she has the chance to meet a blood relative she thought was dead.

Or maybe I'm just seeing what I want to see in her face, trying to make myself feel better.

"So what happened?" she asks me, her arms crossed over her chest.

The twins look to me. I huff out a breath and sit back down. "Hook and I have always been at war, sometimes for no other reason than to torment one another. When I brought Wendy to the island, Roc was here visiting Vane. My rule—about not touching a Darling—had always pertained to me and the Lost Boys. Roc was not about to follow my rules, and Wendy, as we've established, was a brat like you. Determined. Fierce. Easy to fall for."

Her face softens until I tell her the rest.

"Hook took her from me. He obviously didn't want me to retrieve my shadow and he had always tried fucking with the Darlings to keep me from the information.

"It was at that time that Roc cut off Hook's hand and I helped him do it."

Darling's eyes are wide as she digests the story.

"We got Wendy back, but something had changed. Something between her and Roc. He asked her to stay, she said no, and so I took her back.

"Except on the journey to the mortal realm, I took a wrong turn and ended up in Everland. We were quickly surrounded. Leaving her was an easy decision. I had no allegiance to her. And it was her family that took my shadow in the first place. I wanted my revenge against the Darlings and this was an easy, albeit cruel, way of getting it."

Darling drops onto the couch between Bash and Kas and puts her face in her hands. "I can't believe you just left her."

"Have you met him?" Bash says with a laugh.

"It doesn't matter now," I answer. "We can use it to our advantage. If I'd taken her back to the mortal realm, she'd be dead and useless to us now."

Darling looks up at me. "So you're going to use her as a bargaining chip?"

I scowl at her. "Yes. Exactly that."

She huffs and drops back against the couch, half on Kas's arm. Kas shifts to meet her and I am immediately envious of him.

"Promise me we'll get her back then," Darling says.

"We won't have to. Roc will do it for us."

"Promise me, Pan." She clenches her teeth so each word comes out sharp and long.

"Fine. Yes. If Roc doesn't get to her first. But not until I get my shadow."

"Of course." She nods. "And speaking of your shadow…"

I can feel it prowling the island, but it's a vague feeling, like being distantly aware of a ghost in a house. I know it's within the boundaries of Neverland, but I don't exactly know where.

The only thing I'm certain of is that it's not in my territory. If it was, it'd be close enough that I'd fully sense it.

"We have to wait," I tell Darling. "Until tomorrow night, apparently, when Hook has granted us access to his territory."

"Why not just go there now?"

I pin her with a gaze. "Because I can no longer risk war with him."

I think she senses the things I've left unsaid.

If I push Hook too far, he'll come for my Darling girl.

Over my dead fucking body.

I need to play by his rules—for now.

"Aren't you worried he'll find your shadow before then?" she asks.

"Even if he does, I highly doubt he could claim it."

"Because he's just a mortal man?"

"Of a sort." I push off the chair again and fetch the steel case of cigarettes from the bar. I light one, relishing the burn in my lungs. "In the meantime, let's party so I can forget about all of this."

Bash gets up. "Now you're talking."

"No girls," Darling warns.

All three of us look at her and nod.

There she is giving me orders again.

And I'm the asshole that's beginning to follow them.

22

CHERRY

For being immortal men, Pan and the twins and Vane have never been very good at noticing when I'm eavesdropping. They only notice me when it benefits them.

Apparently, I can add Winnie to that list too. I thought she was my friend but I guess not.

When they start down the stairs, I duck into the hallway out of sight.

They want to trade me back to my brother. They think I can get them what they want. Peter Pan and his dumb shadow.

Pan is the only one of the house I haven't slept with. He's no Vane, but I wouldn't have turned him down if he ordered me to my knees. And now Winnie has him, all of them, all to herself. How many men can one girl have?

It isn't fair. But I'm not going to cry about it. Much.

Maybe I can stay. I mean...they told me I could leave a long time ago and I didn't. So why do I have to go now? It isn't like Jas wants me back anyway.

No one seems to want me.

I hurry to my room intending to get dressed up for the bonfire, but when I push inside and flick on the light, something dark shoots across the room.

I yelp and duck as it slams into the door rattling the hinges.

"Oh my god. Is that—" It lunges at me and swipes a sharp claw-like hand across my arm, breaking open the skin. "Hey!"

It lunges again and I whip the door open, race out, and slam it shut, yanking hard on the knob as the door rattles.

"Holy berries and balls," I whisper and look over my shoulder and down the hall both ways. Did anyone just see that?

That's a Neverland shadow. That's a Neverland shadow!

The door rattles again and I wipe the stupid grin off my face. Can it get out of a closed room? Can it travel through cracks and crevices? Does it know how to open a door?

When it goes quiet, I let go of the knob and step back, heart hammering against my eardrums.

I raise my arm to a slant of light from the lanterns and find blood welling in the cut. I swipe the blood away with my fingertip and wipe it on my dark blue jeans.

That thing is brutal. And it's—

I need to tell Vane. When I tell him I have the shadow trapped he'll see I'm useful after all. Maybe he'll even be a little impressed.

Making sure the door is still shut tight, I hurry down the hall and out of the house.

23

HOOK

How hard is it to find one fucking shadow?

From the edge of my balcony, I can see the trees rustling in the forest below and the glow of torch light as the men scour the woods. They have yet to find Pan's shadow.

All incompetent idiots, if you ask me. Peter Pan is due to arrive here tomorrow night. I need to have his shadow before then. I glance in the direction of his territory and can just make out the cut of Marooner's Rock against the moonlit sky.

I hate Peter Pan. It is a hate that thuds in my chest like a bad dream. Sometimes I get caught in a fantasy of what it would feel like to shove my hook into his gut. I detest the sight of my own blood, but Peter Pan's I'll gladly watch gush out of him.

Leaving the balcony, I return to my office and start straightening the items on my desk to distract myself from the sheer frustration of not seeing results. I like my quill clean and returned to its case, the ink pot stoppered with the crystal cut top bought from one of the other islands when we were actively sailing.

I straighten the stack of books on the edge of the desk, line up the spines, and some of the frustration ebbs out.

When I look up, I spot Smee in the doorway. She has that look on her face like she's just consumed a sin she wishes to purge.

"What is it?" I ask and cross the room to my bar when I spot a smudge on one of the glasses.

Smee comes into the room and shuts the door. Her boots are heavy on the worn wood. "One of my spies in the fae palace has just sent me a message."

I already don't like where this is going.

One of the reasons why I wanted Smee back when Pan took her, when I had to make the difficult decision to give away my sister in exchange for Smee, was because of her ability to get where others can't.

She has spies all over Neverland and the Seven Isles.

There is only one person she can never get her eyes on.

I suppose all things considered, that's a very high success rate.

"Spit it out, Smee."

She paces out to the balcony and positions herself in the square of light spilling from the open door. The balcony is my private space and so we are always alone here. Smee leans into the railing and lights a cigarillo, letting the sweet smoke puff out of her full lips. She leaves it there, hanging from her mouth as she hooks her elbows over the railing. The ocean air sends the tail of her bandana flapping at the crown of her head.

The suspense is killing me. Smee knows it. It's her clever, subtle way of putting me in my place. I suppose I have to respect her for it.

"Smee," I say, her name vibrating on my gnashed teeth.

"Tilly has summoned the Crocodile."

If it were possible for a man to lose every ounce of blood with nothing but bad news, I think I would be wrung dry. Nothing but a husk of a man.

I'm cold and numb.

A gentleman such as me should have no weaknesses and yet I have three.

At least one of them is dead. If only the other two were as well.

I turn away from her and rearrange the glasses on the bar, then pick up the smudged one and polish it on the edge of my shirt. "What about your spies on the isles?"

"I heard from one at the port of Summerland that the Crocodile arrived there two days ago and left quickly after."

I close my eyes and summon a breath to stop the burn of vomit at the center of my throat. It would be poor form to vomit all over my bar.

My residual limb throbs and so does the space where my hand used to be. The pain is a ghost I can never exorcise.

Fucking Crocodile.

It's been years since I faced him but I can conjure an image of him as if he were burned to my retinas.

He is cut from granite. Hair dark like nightmares. Eyes green like a mamba snake. Just as quick to bite too.

I can hear his voice, the drawl of his laugh. It echoes in my head. Like salt rubbed on stone.

My stomach spins and I quickly fill a glass with rum and sling it back and focus on the burn of the alcohol, the fuzziness that settles over my veins.

The Crocodile is depraved and ungodly.

I will never rest until he's dead.

If only I could get close enough to him to shove a dagger in his heart.

I turn back to Smee. "Double the reward. Tell the men now. Whoever brings me Pan's shadow will be rich by tomorrow night. But only if they find it before then."

24

WINNIE

Pan and Bash and Kas are drunk. *Very* drunk. They're currently shooting rocks out into the ocean in a giant sling-shot. I think they're competing for some kind of prize though it's not clear what it is or how you win it.

All three of them are trying to forget about their problems in the most human way possible.

And as I sit there high up on the shore and watch them drown their sorrows, I feel tugged away from the revelry.

It's easy to slip off.

I follow the path from the house into the woods. I don't have a destination but my feet seem to carry me in the right direction anyway and I'm not entirely surprised to find myself at the edge of the glowing lagoon.

I am, however, surprised to see Vane floating in the water, face toward the sky.

And he's naked.

All of the air surges out of me in an annoying little gasp and I swear my voice echoes over the lagoon.

"You just going to stand there and gape or get in?" Vane says, his eyes still closed, his body still buoyant in the water.

I swallow.

Is this some kind of trick? Like I get in the water and he gets out just to prove some kind of vague point?

I kick off my shoes at the mouth of the path and sink my toes into the cool sand. I want to get in the water so badly it makes my skin itch. But I can't tell if it's the water and the spirits and the magic calling to me or one very dark and broody Death Shadow.

Maybe it doesn't matter.

My movements are frenzied and clumsy as I slip off my dress and my panties because if Vane is naked, I will be too.

Eyes still closed, he doesn't bother to ogle me like most men would and it annoys me more than I'd like to admit. I can't help but feel like a desperate, eager girl dying for one sliver of his attention.

"Do they bite?" I say when my feet hit the water and the spirits of the lagoon twist and turn.

"No," he answers. "Not if they like you."

My heart ka-thuds against my ear drums.

The water is warm at the shore but grows more refreshing the deeper I get. The spirits or mermaids or whatever they are swim back and forth in front of me, tails glowing and twirling like the feathery tails of koi fish.

How far do I go? How close to Vane do I get? Will he even allow me to get close?

The sandy bottom gets colder and colder so I take to swimming once I'm deep enough and the water rushes up around my shoulders, soaking the ends of my hair.

When I'm a few yards off from Vane, I stop and tread water by kicking my feet and dragging my arms back and forth. It reminds me of lazy afternoons on the beach when Mom and I lived in a touristy oceanside town. The beach days were my best memories because Mom always seemed to relax on the sand. She loved letting the sun bake her skin while I took a fistful of sand and let it leak out in a stream over her toes, burying her grain by grain.

Knowing what I know now—that she was pregnant with me on Neverland and that she found solace in the lagoon—makes me recognize the settling in her when we were on the water.

It must have reminded her of the soothing waters of this magical place. Just wading in here in the bright turquoise makes me feel wholly better. In fact, the cut on my foot is no longer throbbing.

Perhaps my mother and I were always trying to return to this place, looking for relief for some ache we could not name.

Vane floats in the center of the lagoon, his cock just cresting the water, and I can't take my eyes off of him. *I* am ogling *him*. He is letting me.

Out of the four of them, he is the biggest by far.

Somehow, I knew he would be. Without thinking, I can hear Starla in the back of my mind. *Big dick energy, that one.* It almost makes me snicker. Mostly because I'm nervous.

As the water laps against Vane, it fills up the deep ridges between his ab muscles and the V along his hips, then flows back out. He may not be as muscular as the twins or Pan, but he more than makes up for it in not having an ounce of body fat. It makes him look more myth than man, as if he were born of the gods themselves.

Finally, he rights himself and whips his head around, shaking the water from his hair. Several fat drops roll down the wavy lines of his scars, down the cut of his cheekbones.

When he faces me, his violet eye reflects the turquoise of the lagoon, making it glow.

The water is still warm but I can't stop shivering and my nipples are so taut it almost hurts.

I've been craving Vane's attention since Pan brought me to Neverland, but now that I have it and have him alone, I don't know what to do with him.

He is bigger than me and I'm not talking size.

Presence. Power. Energy.

It's hard not to be overwhelmed by him and maybe that's why I turn into a sputtering dork.

"It's a nice night. I like swimming. In water. All water really."

Fuck.

What the hell am I doing?

More droplets follow the bridge of his nose and drip from the end. He just stares at me as the water ripples around us. I slow my feet, letting my body sink lower as if I can hide in the water. It sways around my mouth and when a little sneaks in, I don't taste salt. It's clean and crisp.

"Why are you here, Darling?" he asks, his rough voice reverberating across the lagoon.

"I don't know," I admit. "I was drawn here, I think."

He comes closer, running a hand through his hair, and it sticks up along his forehead. I've never seen him this disheveled and it's hot as fuck.

My belly clenches.

"Why are *you* here?" I counter.

"To get away from you."

The dejection is swift and sour.

"Why? What have I done to make you hate me so damn much?"

"I don't understand you," he says and narrows his eyes, comes closer. "I don't like things I don't understand."

"I'm not a thing. I'm a person."

"A naughty Darling girl."

But he doesn't say it like he's teasing. There's pain in his words, like he's afraid of what I might do, what trouble I might get into and I'm immediately reminded of what he said to me the night Tilly got inside my head and he carted me off to safety.

"Where I come from, little girls like you are broken every day for no other reason than to watch them crack. And I'm fucking sick of it."

"Tell me about your island."

He blinks and reels back, suddenly on guard. "Why?"

"Because I want to know where you come from and why you are the way you are."

A glowing shape circles behind him.

"If you're looking for redeeming qualities within me, you'll be disappointed."

"No. I only want the truth."

The shape darts away when Vane sinks back into the water and dips his head, soaking his hair again. "My home island is called Darkland and it is exactly what it sounds like."

A dark land for a Dark One.

"Why did you leave?"

"Because there was nothing left for me there."

"No family?"

Above us, the sky turns dark as thick clouds roll in. The water is suddenly warmer than the air.

"I had a family once," he admits. "Until I didn't."

Oh god.

Maybe there were more clues in what he said to me that night in his bed.

Little girls like you are broken every day...

"Who was she?"

He says nothing again, letting the silence grow weightier between us.

I take a guess. "A sister. You had a sister."

"We did."

"What happened?"

"Some very bad men did some very bad things and then she died." He says it in such a cold, detached tone of voice that I can't help but immediately feel a pang of sympathy for him.

Vane pretends he is unaffected but I think he might feel this pain more than any of the others would.

A lump wedges in my throat and I swallow back twice to try to dislodge it. "That's awful. Truly."

"She's better off dead," he says.

"Could you not...I mean...you have the Death Shadow..."

"I didn't at the time." His brow furrows, his gaze faraway. I know what he's thinking—he couldn't protect her.

"How did you get the shadow?"

"Easy," he says, "I spent three years searching for it and when I found it, I claimed it. And then I gutted every single one of them."

Them. The men who hurt his sister.

"Good," I say with more venom than I intended. "How were you able to claim the shadow? Are you not human?"

He laughs and shakes his head.

Now I'm very curious. "So what are you?"

"Does it matter?"

"Maybe?"

He swims back toward me, cut shoulders moving gracefully in the water. "If I give back my shadow, maybe it will matter then. Maybe I'll tell you."

Frustration bubbles up inside of me. He's cutting me off again. Maybe I should just—

Something skims the bottom of my feet and I yelp and lurch back.

Right into Vane's arms.

My heart gets lodged behind my teeth. Every nerve is blinking brightly. His hands are on my waist, holding me up, and I can feel his strong thighs treading the water beneath us keeping us above the surface.

I'm finding it harder and harder to take a full breath.

"Why do you hate me, Vane?" I ask again, quieter this time. I'm unable to hide the desperation in my voice. I need to know just as much as he wants to figure me out.

"I don't hate you," he admits and levels me with his violet eye. "I dislike the way you make me feel."

"Which is how?"

His gaze drops to my lips as my tongue darts out. "Reckless." He drags me closer and our legs tangle and a thrill slips down my spine. "Dangerous," he adds and frowns at the bruises still marring my throat.

"I told you already once before—"

"Yes, I know Darling. You're stronger than you look."

"I don't need you to protect me," I say, thinking I'm hitting on the past wound of losing his sister.

"I don't want to protect you," he says, his voice rumbling, "I want to fuck you until you tremble beneath me." He guides my legs around his waist, and my opening is lined up with his now hard cock.

I pant out a little mewl of delight.

"So why don't you?" I ask.

"Because those bruises on your neck would be the least of your worries."

"I don't care."

"You'd get no safe word from me."

"Fine. I understand."

"No, you fucking don't."

I'm breathing much too quickly. I think I'm oxygen deprived at this point because I can't think straight, can barely see straight.

"Just fuck me already."

I'm breaking my rule, and Pan's. I'm trying too hard.

The head of Vane's cock teases at my opening and my heart rate picks up.

"Vane," I say on a breath. "Just do—"

He kisses me. And there is nothing soft or kind or gentle about it. His lips are on mine, devouring me. His tongue darts in, claiming the taste of me and a deep growl sounds in his chest.

He grabs my ass, forcing my pussy up to meet his cock and he sinks in an inch.

"Oh my god," I say around his lips because my brain isn't making a single connection to my mouth. This is what I wanted. Every single part of it. I don't care how dangerous he is or how painful it might be or—

He arches my back, bringing my breast above water so he can suck my nipple into his mouth.

Both of his eyes are black and a shiver shakes through my shoulders.

He's rough with me, biting at me, and I cry out at the sky.

When I look back down, blood is swirling in the turquoise water and beading on the peak of my nipple.

With fire in his eyes, Vane drags his tongue over me,

cleaning off the redness and then he nips again, breaking open the skin even more.

The pain catches me off guard and tears spring in my eyes. One escapes, trailing down my cheek.

Vane goes still.

I wiggle my hips, trying to claim more of his cock, but he roughly shoves me off.

"What are you doing?"

"Go." He points me toward the shore.

"What?"

"Get out of the water." He's visibly trembling. "Get out and walk away. Slowly."

"No. I—"

His black hair goes white and his voice takes on a sinister hollowness. "Get the fuck out of here, Darling."

I shrink back.

"Go," he says again. "Right fucking now."

Heart still lodged in my throat, my heart sinking to my navel, I trudge toward shore and then slowly step from the water. Vane is stalking me and goosebumps pop on my arms as I feel him at my back.

The thought of him fighting his inner demons not to claim me makes me wet and tingly.

I scoop up my dress and pull it on over my head and look at him over my shoulder.

He's inching closer. He's telling me to leave, but I don't think his shadow wants me to. Maybe he doesn't either.

"Walk away," he tells me.

"What if I don't want to? I can make my own decisions, you know."

"Darling, I won't tell you again."

I swallow hard and stumble back and he takes three

quick steps closer as if to catch me. Even gone to the shadow, he's still cognizant of my safety.

And it suddenly clicks, the real secret to unraveling Vane.

I was wrong about him, but so was Peter Pan. It's not that I have to try harder or try less. It's that I have to be exactly who I am. Every ugly, broken part.

I have to be vulnerable and maybe that terrifies me most of all.

Show him all of my cracks and let him make his own on my skin.

I have endured.

I can endure him if it's the only way I can have him.

He must read something in my body because he slowly shakes his head, grits his teeth, and says, "*Winnie. Don't.*"

But he couldn't stop me if he tried.

I turn around and run.

25

WINNIE

THE BRANCHES OF THE NEVERLAND FOREST PULL AT MY HAIR AND
scratch at my face.

But I keep running.

Vane is faster than I anticipated and I can feel the earth
shaking beneath his feet as he gives me chase and draws
nearer.

The terror settles in as I round a grove of trees.

It's a clawing terror that erupts from my throat in
useless, shaky gasps. Tears well in my eyes, clouding my
vision and my shoulder slams into the skinny trunk of a
birch tree.

He is silent as he chases me. And my heart is beating so
fast in anticipation, I can feel it drumming in my teeth.

He's going to catch me.

He's going to catch me.

How long do I run?

How far?

I look over my shoulder and find him just a few feet

behind me. He's gone to the dark shadow now. Or maybe there is no separation between them, only determination.

The terror squeezes my heart and makes it skip several beats, then flutter hard like it's about to explode.

Goosebumps rise on my arms and a shiver races down my spine and my chest is too tight and my breathing too shallow and—

He snatches me around the waist and slams me against the trunk of a tree. The bark bites into my back and the wind is knocked out of me. I'm tingling between my legs in hot anticipation of what he might do to me.

His hand comes to my throat as his weight sinks over top of me and he kicks my legs apart. His cock finds the pocket between my thighs and rubs against me, forcing a high-pitched moan from my lips.

"Is this what you wanted, Darling?" he asks in that hollow, vibrating voice that belongs to the shadow, which makes the hair at the nape of my neck stand up straight. "I told you not to run."

It's hard to think straight inside of the terror. There is only the base instinct to run and cry and beg. But I fight it. Giving in is the only way to meet him in the dark.

Shaking, sobbing, I wind my legs around his waist as the terror pulses on the edges of my vision. "This is... exactly...what I wanted." I have to take several hiccupping breaths between words.

"You don't know what the fuck you're asking for."

"Then show me."

With a growl, he rips off my dress, tearing it into scraps of fabric.

The darkness of the Death Shadow surges around his eyes like an inky mask and the terror doubles in my veins, stealing the exhilaration.

Fuck, fuck.

Focus.

There must be a way to fight that effect. I don't want to be terrified. I want to be fucking high on the pleasure of having him.

His cock slides up my wetness, hitting my throbbing clit, and I squeeze my eyes shut, purging the unspent tears.

I'm so terrified, my head is pounding. I want to crawl out of my skin. I want to fight and run.

Vane is an ocean wave pulling me deeper and deeper.

He rocks his hips back, stealing the heat of his cock before he shoves it in roughly, causing me to cry out.

He's so fucking big it hurts on impact and my teeth clack together.

"I will split this wet cunt in two," he says. "You'll be begging me to stop."

"No, I won—"

He sinks inside of me, filling me up, and then brings both hands to my throat and squeezes.

My eyes automatically bug out.

He fucks me. Hard. Fast. Brutally. The tree rattles above us.

There is no air, no air to beg, and tears stream down my face.

He is relentless.

Consuming.

Fucking me and fucking me as his teeth gnash together and his black eyes spark with life.

How did...how do I...

I can't breathe. My vision tunnels. His grip tightens.

Fuck.

Fuck.

I am in too deep.

I didn't know what I was doing.

He tried to warn me.

I didn't listen.

I'm going to die here.

My hands scramble for purchase. That base instinct trying to escape.

And then my fingers close on a tiny, sharp branch just overhead.

Pain.

I need pain.

I break off the branch with a snap and with every ounce of energy I have left, I stab the end into my palm and drag it across the meaty flesh. The pain is sharp and immediate and every muscle clenches up.

The terror vanishes, overrun by the sharp agony in my palm. I grab one of Vane's hands still around my throat. I pull and slap at him as the darkness creeps into my vision and then suddenly he's blinking, staring at the blood as it runs down my chest, as it fills the divots along his fingernails.

"Darling." His voice is hoarse, and his grip loosens, but his eyes are still black.

I come back into my body as oxygen fills my lungs in one deep, body-shaking gasp.

"Fuck me," I tell him and inhale deeply. "Fuck me now."

His hands sink to my ass, spreading me, and he fills me back up. Every inch of him, every hard ridge. He pulls back out, slamming back in with enough force to make the tree groan.

"Oh yes, fuck," I say and wrap my arms around his neck and hang on for dear life.

There is nothing gentle about him. He's still consumed

by darkness, but he has control of it and me and he's taking what I'm freely giving.

And it feels so fucking good.

"Rub that pussy for me, Darling," he says and slams us against the tree again. "I'm so fucking close to spilling inside of you."

"Yeah?"

"Yes," he says on a growl.

I reach down between us and swirl two fingers over my clit and immediately toe the edge. "Oh, shit. I don't want to come yet."

I want to linger. I want to savor this. Every second of it.

Vane is mine. He's mine and I'm his and I'm never going to let him push me away ever again.

I hold my fingers tightly against my clit as if that will ward off the pleasure threatening to pound through me.

Eyes squeezed tight, I lay my head back against the tree as Vane punishes me with his cock.

"Winnie," he says. "You'll make that wet pussy come for me and you'll do it now."

"I don't want to," I say on a moan.

"Look at me," he orders and I pry my eyes open. The blackness has receded from his gaze, and his violet eye is glittering with heat and desire and need. He needs me and he needs this and more than anything in the world, I want to give it to him.

Vane will always be the last person to demand anything from me and he will always be the one I want to please the most because of it.

"Okay," I say.

He grabs my hand and captures two of my fingers in his mouth. He sucks me with his lips, circles my fingertips with his tongue, soaking me before guiding my hand back down to my clit.

"Let me have you, Win," he says. "Let me fill up that wet cunt while you scream my name."

"Yeah. *Yes*." I moan loudly as I soak my clit with his spit. I'm so wet, it's dripping down his balls as he sinks into me all the way to the hilt.

I have him.

I have him.

I barely have to touch myself before I'm flying over the edge, my voice echoing through the woods. "Oh my god. Vane! Fuck! Vane!" He pounds into me. Fast. Relentless. Giving my pussy the fucking it deserves.

He's growing harder, more frenzied with his movements, and then he's grunting into me, spilling inside of me. "Fuck, Win," he says on a growl, his cock throbbing against my clenched inner walls.

Thunder rumbles overhead.

He growls through his teeth, pumps more into me, his fingers now bruising on the backs of my thighs.

I pant for several breaths as my soul floats back into my body. "Oh my god," I say again. "That was…" I have no words. I don't know how any word could sum it up.

Vane rocks in and out of me in slow, languid thrusts, like he's savoring the feel of me still wrapped around his cock.

"You weren't supposed to run," he says and leans forward resting his forehead against mine. Our breath mingles.

"I'm glad I did."

"I could have killed you." He slides in again, still impossibly hard for having already came.

"But you didn't."

"You think you've won something."

"No," I say and press my lips against his. His mouth is unmoving for all of a second before he's kissing me back. "I claimed something. I claimed you."

He growls against my mouth and I feel his cock straining inside of me. "You keep thinking that."

"I did. You're mine now. And there's no turning back."

He digs his hips into me, sinking the head of his cock all the way to my uterus, I swear to god.

"Perhaps you have gone mad, after all."

I kiss him again, more deeply this time and his tongue slides against mine. I thread my fingers through his still damp hair as thunder rumbles again. When I pull back, I tell him, "Don't deny me ever again."

"Needy little Darling."

"Fucking right, I am."

He presses in. "Make me a promise."

"Anything."

"So fucking eager it annoys me."

"Shut up and tell me."

His mouth trails over my jaw, then down my bruises, my raw throat. "If I ever lose control, promise me you'll knee me in the balls or stab me in the face."

"I will never do that—"

"Promise me," he says on a growl and drags his teeth over the sensitive flesh just beneath my ear. I yip in surprise and shrink in on myself. "Promise me, Darling. It's the only way you get me."

I sigh. "Fine. I promise to stab you in the face."

He finally pulls out of me and I pout up at him as my feet hit the forest floor. We're both naked and without clothes.

"I have a shirt you can have on the beach," he tells me and pushes me back toward the lagoon.

I realize too late the mistake I've made.

He has a clear view of my back.

He grabs me by the arms and pulls me to a stop. The air is charged and silent until Vane inhales and says on a growl, "Darling, who did that to you?"

I whirl around, giving him my front, but he takes me by the shoulders and spins me back again. His fingertips ghost over the scars and I couldn't stop the shiver that overtakes me even if I tried.

"Who?" he repeats. "Give me a name so that I can cut the skin from their bones."

"It was no one."

"Winnie."

"It was my mom!"

His hand splays over the base of my neck, fingers curling over my shoulder. I sense his stillness and his reluctance.

"Merry did this to you?"

"Not directly. She hired people to do it."

"She paid money for this?"

The anger makes his voice vibrate and when I turn back to him, his eyes are black once again.

"When Pan finds out—"

"He already knows."

"Then why didn't you tell me?"

"I don't know. I didn't want your pity. I wanted your respect." As soon as the admission is out, my face blooms with embarrassment. I hadn't meant to say so much.

When his face falls, I immediately regret letting the words spill out. "You wanted my respect so you let me pound you against a tree instead?"

The blush intensifies. "Maybe. I don't know."

He steers me toward the beach again as lightning chases a rumble of thunder overhead. When we come back out on the lagoon, he scoops up his black t-shirt and bunches it up in his hands so all I have to do is stick my head in and let him thread my arms through the sleeves. I drown in it once it settles over my body and I think he appreciates the sight more than he'd like because he can't stop staring at me. He won't stare at my naked body, but he'll enjoy the sight of me in his clothes.

I've never been self-conscious until now.

I fold my arms over my middle, digging my toe into the cool sand.

"We should have never sent Merry back once we knew she was pregnant," he says. "We should have never let her raise you alone."

I scoff. "What, and keep her here? So you all could help raise me? That sounds creepy and worse."

He looks away, knowing I'm right.

"I firmly believe that everything happens for a reason and I was where I was supposed to be." He glances back at me, violet eye bright. "And now I'm exactly where I'm supposed to be once again."

He yanks up his pants, tucks his cock inside. He must smell like me and that gives me a ridiculous little flare of joy. "Where you're *supposed* to be is home," he says and shoves me toward the path once he's buttoned his pants. "You're shivering and it's late and now you're bruised even more."

I grin up at him. "I like you being rough with me. "

"Stop it."

"I'm allowed to like it."

He grumbles. "Not at the expense of the oxygen in your lungs."

"Mmm, speak for yourself. I wouldn't mind experimenting with that under controlled circumstances."

"You want me to choke you?" He scowls over at me.

I think about it a second. "Yes."

"Fucking hell, Darling." He puts his hand at the small of my back and gives me another push like he's aghast at this idea. "Get back to the house. Before I give you exactly what you want."

26

CHERRY

I CAN'T CATCH MY BREATH I'M CRYING SO HARD.

Vane gave in to her.

He gave in to her?!

I run through the woods. I don't know which direction I'm going but it doesn't matter. Vane gave in to Winnie and the look on his face—

I didn't mean to spy. I spy a lot, but I didn't mean to spy on them. I was looking for Vane and then I heard him and when I stumbled through the woods and saw them—

The tears come fast, streaming down my face.

All of the years I've been in the house and I've tried everything and I even caught the shadow and thought—

I come to a stop on the road, the one that leads between Darlington Port and the house. I look down at my arm, at the cut now crusted over with dried blood.

I caught the shadow. I have that dark, dangerous shadow trapped in my room.

And if a Darling girl were to stumble in there—

Okay, no, I can't do that.

That would be wrong.

Vane's face flashes through my mind as he fucked Winnie against that tree. He was enjoying it. She has him wrapped around her finger now. He's never going to give in to me if she's around.

Hands balled into fists, I yell at the sky. "This is all so fucking stupid!"

But it feels like my insides are trying to crawl up my throat. My stomach is in knots and my eyes are burning and my throat is clogged and—

Vane is supposed to be *mine*.

And Winnie was supposed to go back to her world and stay there.

I don't believe in coincidences.

I dry my eyes on the sleeve of my shirt and make my way back to the house.

Maybe the universe gave me the shadow for a reason.

Maybe I'm supposed to use it after all.

27

PETER PAN

THE TWINS ARE LAUGHING AND THEY CAN'T STOP.

"You launched that fucker to the clouds," Bash says.

Kas wipes tears from his face as the ocean breeze blows his hair in his face. "Did you see him pinwheeling all the way down?"

The Lost Boy in question, the one I stuck in the giant slingshot and launched into the sky is trudging back up the beach, his clothes soaking wet and hanging off of his scrawny body like moss from a tree. He's drunk too. We're all drunk.

I needed this more than I realized.

"That was fun," the Lost Boy says and smiles up at me.

"Great," I tell him. "Now get the fuck out of here."

He hurries back up to the fire where the rest of the Lost Boys are drinking, playing cards, and cavorting with the town girls.

Bash and Kas and I have been noticeably absent from the fireside.

Inevitably, girls will circle us and we'll have to turn them down and I don't want them to ruin my good time.

I scan the crowd for *my* girl, but she's noticeably absent too.

"Where's our Darling?" I ask the twins.

Bash hands me a freshly uncorked bottle of rum. "I think I saw her go into the house a while ago."

The urge to go to her is nearly unbearable.

But there's something I need to say to the twins while I have them alone. I take a long pull from the amber bottle, then hand it off to one of them. "What did your sister offer you?"

They look at one another and I can hear the chime of bells over the crashing of the ocean. "No, fuckers. You speak to my face."

Bash sighs. "In a vague sort of way, she offered us our wings back and the possibility of being welcomed back to court if we sided with her or gave her something she could use against you."

Tilly may be young compared to me, but I have to give her credit—she knows how to motivate her brothers. They may pretend like being banished is but a distant memory, but I know it is a splinter wedged deep beneath the skin, one they pick and pick at as the wound festers and the skin rots.

This business with Tilly, losing their wings, leaving their home, it's unresolved business, and the longer they ignore it, the worse it'll get.

"I don't have the power to get you your wings directly," I say, "but if I have my shadow, I'll have the power to help you stage a coup if that's what you want."

They pretend like they're just considering this offer, but they're not stupid. This was always the way it would go down. I think in some way I always knew they would eventually end up on the throne. Maybe that's why I took them in when they were banished. They always held some value to me, but now I've come to see them as brothers.

Little asshole brothers, anyway.

The tinkling of bells punctuates the night. I let them have their secret conversation this time.

"All right," Kas finally says. "Consider this our official word. We'll stand by your side if you help us get our wings and the court back."

I nod, feeling the last vestiges of the alcohol burn off. As an immortal, I can never stay drunk long enough.

"I think we'll enjoy this," I say. "Overthrowing the fae queen has a certain ring to it."

Bash snorts. "That's still our sister you're talking about."

"Apologies." I hook my arms around their necks and tug them into me. "Let me correct that. Overthrowing your sister will be fun."

Kas's yanks his hair out from beneath my arm. "You really are the world's biggest asshole."

"Now we're on the same page."

28

WINNIE

When we reach the house, Pan is in the foyer. "There you are. Where the fuck have you two been?"

"Fucking," I say proudly.

Vane groans.

Pan's gaze darts between us and I notice he gets caught on the fresh bruises around my throat. "Are you all right?" he asks.

"I am magnificent."

"Quit bragging," Vane says. "It does not become you."

"On the contrary. It becomes me very well."

"Bash," Pan yells through the house.

"Yeah?" Bash answers from the loft.

"Get the salve." Pan points a finger at me. "You'll use it this time. End of discussion."

I roll my eyes, but there's only so much I can get away with, with these powerful men. "Fine."

We go up the winding staircase and Bash meets us with

the salve in hand. He narrows his eyes at Vane. "You didn't break our little Darling, did you, Dark One?"

"No," I answer.

"Debatable," Vane says.

Pan grabs the salve and comes over to me, but Vane snatches it from his grip and then hooks me around the waist and steers me toward his room.

"Vane!" Pan yells.

But Vane keeps pushing me and says, "She's mine tonight."

"I didn't know we could call dibs on the Darling," Bash says, his voice fading away as Vane guides me into his room and shuts the door behind us.

This is the first time I'm in his room *and* coherent enough to take it in. He goes around and lights several lanterns and the golden light spills across the room.

The space is half what I expected, half not.

The bed is large, the four posts thick with delicate carvings on the headboard and the footboard. The bed is made with a soft linen duvet and several thick pillows.

Across from the bed is a fireplace, the stone hearth cold in the middle of Neverland's warm season. On the mantle is a stack of books, a tiny model ship, and several other trinkets.

And hanging above the fireplace is a giant oil painting of a meadow with a girl standing in the center, her white dress caught in the wind.

She's facing away from the viewer, so it's impossible to know what she looks like or what she's thinking, but the looseness in her body leads me to believe she's happy.

"Sit," Vane orders, so I go to the bed and sit on the edge. He uncorks the salve and nudges my chin up with the hard ridge of his knuckle and then dips his fingers into the green goo. His touch is gentle as he rubs it into my skin and when the warmth sinks in, my eyes slip closed and I exhale.

"Better?" he asks.

My eyes pop open and it takes me a second to refocus on him. He's rimmed in the light, a dark vision, spun in gold. He's still shirtless, all hard lines and solid muscle. His size is overwhelming and also somehow comforting. As if I will always be protected as long as he's near.

The realization of that, of how he makes me feel, catches in my throat and comes out sounding like a gasp.

"What is it?" he asks.

"Nothing, it's just..."

He patiently waits for me to answer.

"I'm worried that this is some kind of illusion, like maybe the twins are tricking me into thinking you're here. And I'm terrified that it will end."

I know how I must sound. Like a pathetic, needy girl desperate for the Dark One's attention and his cock. He fucks me once and I can't get enough of him.

But it's all true.

More than Pan, more than Bash and Kas, I wanted Vane because I recognize something in him that feels familiar.

We are both broken and so fucking afraid that someone will notice.

"Up," he orders and I lurch to my feet. He sets the salve aside and yanks back the duvet. "Get in."

I hurry into his bed, my heart picking up speed in my chest, butterflies hammering at my navel. He slides in next to me and pulls me into him, then tucks the blanket around us.

I am so happy it hurts. Surrounded by his scent, nestled in his arms.

I don't want the bubble to burst.

I don't want to cry like an idiot.

"I am here," he says, his voice raspy at my ear as he holds me at his side, his fingers trailing up my arm. "Do you feel that?"

"Yes." I shiver beneath him.

"I am here and I am real and I'm not going anywhere."

I recall Pan telling me Vane was considering returning to his island. I'm not sure if Vane knows I know, but I decide to use it to my advantage.

Vane strikes me as the type of person who does not give promises easily because he always stands by his word.

"Promise me you aren't going anywhere."

He grumbles.

"You forced me to promise to stab you in the face. Now give me this. Please."

"Fine. I promise, Darling."

"Promise what?"

"That I'm not going anywhere."

Those words echo in my head as the fairy salve soaks into my bloodstream and eases all of the tension and ache from my body.

I hold on to those words with everything I have. And hold on to him with just a little more.

29

HOOK

"Jas."

A hand grips my shoulder and shakes.

I lurch awake and come out swinging with my hook and just barely catch Smee across the face with the sharp, curved tine. She dodges at the last second and frowns at me with enough disappointment to scorch eyebrows.

As if that was my fault.

"Christ." I scrub at my eyes with thumb and forefinger. "Don't do that."

"How am I to wake you then, eh? With a ten-foot pole?"

"Perhaps so, if you'd like to keep your face connected to your skull." When I look up at her, she's tense with impatience. "What is it?"

"They found Pan's shadow."

I lurch to my feet. "Smee! You should have led with that."

She mutters some obscenities behind me as I rush from the house.

"Where?" I call over my shoulder.

"Down by the river's edge."

Mysterious River is northeast of the house, but just a short distance away. I can hear the rush of water against the river bed as I approach and the men shouting at one another.

"Out of my way!" I yell and shove several pirates aside.

Backed against the trunk of an oak tree is Peter Pan's shadow.

It's hard to see it when you look at it directly as it's more suggestion than shape. But I can feel it. The air vibrates with power.

For the first time in a long time, I am alive with hope.

The look on the Crocodile's face when he realizes I possess the Neverland shadow...

"Now what, Captain?" one of the men asks.

Excellent question. I never thought the plan through to this point. Perhaps I was a bit too reckless in that regard.

How does one capture a rogue shadow?

Better yet, how does one claim it?

I look to Smee. She's spent some years on the other islands studying magic. She's mortal and landed in the isle chain when she was just nineteen. But she's always been fascinated with this stuff and has a memory to rival all.

"No one who has a shadow has ever been forthcoming with how to claim it," she says.

"Bloody hell."

The shadow darts to the side and all of us surge to corral it. It swings back to the tree and leaps into an elbow between branches.

"I need a chest," I tell them.

No one moves.

"Well, don't just bloody well stand there!"

Two men rush off into the woods, back to the house. I inch toward it.

"Careful, Jas," Smee says.

"I know what I'm doing."

The edges of the shadow vibrate as I reach out with my hook. If it's violent, my metal can take the hit. The rest of me can't.

I've heard some nasty things about the Dark Shadow and it's difficult to predict what the Life Shadow will do.

It bounces back and forth, stretching long.

The men return with a trunk the size of a large dog.

"Open it," I order them. "And hold it up."

They position themselves, one on either side of the chest, one hand on the bottom, the other on the lid, so the chest is a gaping hole in front of the shadow.

I don't need to know how to claim it right this second, but I can't let it out of my grasp.

"Get ready to close the lid," I tell them and stalk behind the tree.

Smee circles around the other side, her arms loose at her sides, knees bent ready to spring.

"On three," I tell her.

"Aye," she says.

"One," I say.

The pirates go still.

"Two."

The men holding the chest fidget and I shoot them a murderous look.

They right it again, holding it steady.

"Three!"

Smee and I lunge and the shadow springs forward and thunks hard into the bottom of the chest. The men drop it and it teeters on its bottom edge. "Close it, you idiots!"

The burlier of the two jumps on the lid as the shadow thumps on the underside trying to get out while the second man pops in the latch.

Once it's secure, I finally breathe, and then I look at Smee and smile.

She shakes her head. "I don't like this, Jas."

"I don't pay you to like things, Smee. Just to find them. Now come on. Let us figure out how to claim the damn thing before Peter Pan arrives."

30

WINNIE

We're all in the loft waiting for the Never King to wake.

Tonight is the night he'll go to Hook's territory and search for his shadow. They all seem confident he'll find it.

Vane is sitting in the corner of the couch reading a book. My head is in his lap and I'm stretched out the length of the couch with Bash nestled between my thighs. He takes in a deep breath of my scent and his eyes roll back in his head.

"You smell so good, Darling," he says. "Mind if I have a taste?"

"I'm full of Vane's cum," I tell him. "But go ahead."

"For fuck's sake," Vane says on a grumble.

He's finally given in to me, but he's still not quite happy about it which makes me doubly happy.

"I'm hungry," Bash says, "but not *that* hungry." He resettles between my legs and I run my fingers through his dark, silky hair.

Across the room, Kas is in one of the leather chairs, legs kicked over the arm while he tries to solve one of those little wooden novelty puzzles. His brow is furrowed, his focus unshakeable. He has the same determined look on his face from when I was tied to the Never Tree and he was wrenching orgasm after orgasm out of me.

It's hard to believe that this is my new reality. That I have four insanely hot men all to myself. That they not only want to fuck me, but also seem to like me for exactly who I am.

And who I'm not.

Could this be my life from now on? Just lazing on the beach and fucking any one of them whenever I want? Letting Bash cook me food while Kas tells me a story and Vane broods beside me while Peter Pan smokes a cigarette and looks sexier than any man has a right to look.

I want it to be my reality so badly it makes my stomach hurt.

As the sun goes down, my anticipation grows and when I hear the door on Pan's tomb clank open, I get an excited swirl in my belly.

"Got it," Kas says and holds up the reassembled wooden puzzle, looking pleased with himself.

"Well done, brother," Bash says as he hooks his arm around my thigh. "You solved a children's toy."

"Oh, shut the fuck up," Kas says.

"Both of you shut the fuck up."

The Never King has awoken.

God, he is hot.

He's shirtless and his pants hang low on his hips, exposing the cut lines that dip down below the waistband of his pants. Like Vane, he's not as bulky as the twins, but he's easily the tallest and his presence takes up the most space.

We're all a little enamored with him, I think. Even Vane.

I look up from Vane's lap and Pan meets my gaze and the wrinkle between his brows smooths out when he takes in the relaxed sight of us, like he's been carrying the tension between Vane and me in that space between his eyes.

I don't know why, but his relief at seeing us all getting along makes me feel something deep in my chest that almost feels like warmth.

Please let this be real.

"Get up, all of you," he says. "We have somewhere to be."

"Me too?" I ask.

"You'll stay nearby but out of sight with the twins. I'm not leaving you here alone for Hook to send his men along to steal you."

Kas and Bash are shirtless and in shorts—their normal beach attire—so they get up and disappear down the hall to get dressed.

"Bash make coffee?" Pan asks.

"Yes," I answer.

"You two come with me." He heads into the kitchen.

I get up. Vane shuts his book and sets it aside and rises beside me. He gives me a long, lingering look that makes my insides quake and my scalp tingle.

Then he pushes me toward the kitchen.

Pan is at the counter filling a clay mug with hot coffee. Steam rises from the pot. "Tell me how you are," he says, but he doesn't make it clear who he's referring to.

Vane leans his back against the edge of the counter and folds his arms over his chest.

"I'm fine," I answer. "Better than fine."

Cup in hand, Pan turns to me. His eyes go to my throat, then roam over my body as if checking for lies. When he seems satisfied with what he finds, he cuts to Vane. "You figured it out then?"

"Yes," Vane replies.

Pan doesn't ask for specifics and I admire his confidence in letting us keep our secrets.

I should have known that the way to the Dark One's heart was through pain and blood. But most of all, *vulnerability*.

Vane and I understand each other because we are both broken.

And both of us hate to admit it.

So we won't.

We will tell those truths in sex and pain and blood until we're both satiated.

Pan nods at us and then sips from his coffee. The steam stretches across the sharp planes of his face and I'm envious of its proximity to him.

I know he has a mission to fulfill, a shadow to claim, but I am suddenly hungry for him too.

"We'll leave soon," Pan says. "Put on more clothes, Darling," he adds. "Only we get to appreciate you."

"You mean we're not going to add Captain Hook to our harem?" I tease.

Both Pan and Vane scowl like I just suggested we add an octopus. "Do not utter those words ever again," Vane says on a grumble.

Pan tips his cup at Vane. "I will second that. Now go, Darling. Ten minutes."

"All right. Fine." I start to walk away, but Pan snatches me by the wrist and yanks me back into him. He plants his lips on mine but opens wide so his tongue can dart into my mouth and meet my own.

I shiver even though his body burns hot next to mine.

When he pulls away, he nudges me toward Vane.

And Vane takes the challenge.

He spins me so my back is to his chest and then hooks one arm around my waist, while the other hand is curled around my throat. He turns me up to him and claims my mouth with his, his tongue sinking deeper into me than Pan's ever did.

I cling to his arm, trying to keep myself upright as my head spins and my breathing quickens. My pussy is buzzing for attention and Vane lifts his hand to my breast and squeezes it hard, finishing on my nipple with a pinch so acute, I moan into his mouth.

When he ends the kiss and rights me, I'm dizzy and delirious and swaying on my feet.

Pan licks his lips, clearly liking the show. But for once, he's more focused on his mission than he is on my pussy. "Go on," he says and tips his head toward my room.

Maybe when we get back, I can have them both, the Death Shadow and the Life Shadow.

Oh god, just the thought of them both filling me up is orgasmic. I won't last five minutes with these brutal men.

As I leave the room, I make sure to put extra sway into my hips.

I want them to know exactly what they have to look forward to after this mission.

31

PETER PAN

Vane and I watch our Darling leave the room like she's the sun setting below the horizon, taking her warmth with her.

If I get my shadow back, I can return to the daylight, but perhaps Darling has been all the light I've needed.

"You really have it tamed?" I ask Vane.

He blinks away from Darling's retreating figure. "Tamed enough." Then he frowns. "I need pain and blood to reel it back in, it would seem."

That makes sense. But I still don't like it.

"I'll give it back," he adds. "I don't want or need the shadow anymore. I'll give it back..."

I sense he's trailed off and left something unsaid.

"You'll give it back for her."

He scoffs and looks away but doesn't deny it.

Darling has us all worshipping her. I still don't know how she managed it. She is a magician pulling tricks and yet I've yet to see the reveal.

Perhaps her wet pussy is the trick and the flourish

because fuck if I don't feel awed by her every single time she's wrapped around my cock.

"I don't know how the Life Shadow felt," he says, "but the Dark Shadow aches. It is a burden I no longer wish to bear. That's the end of it. It will be good to be without it."

"And the Neverland Dark Shadow?" I ask. "What shall we do with it?"

"Give it to one of the twins."

"Kas could probably handle it. He's practical. Patient. Reliable. I feel like out of the two, he'd handle it better."

"I would agree."

"But you'll keep yours until we overthrow the fae queen, yeah? Do it for me."

It's not phrased as a question, but I think he knows it's not an order either.

"I won't leave us vulnerable. But my brother coming to the island will complicate things. It'll drudge up our past."

"I know." But I don't really. I don't know their story, just the outline of it and even that's fuzzy.

"One problem at a time," I repeat.

"Too many fucking problems." He pushes away from the island. "Speaking of problems—have you seen Cherry? If we show up on Hook's doorstep without her, we might have an issue."

"I haven't seen her. She'll turn up eventually and then we'll shoo her home like a feral cat."

He nods. "Let's go bust some pirate ass then and get your shadow back. I'm tired of being the most powerful one of the group."

"Fucking asshole," I say on a laugh and hook him around the neck. He laughs. "When I have it back, let's race through the clouds."

His violet eye lights up with the promise of a challenge. "I will enjoy beating you."

32

KAS

WE WALK TO HOOK'S TERRITORY, OUR DARLING TUCKED SAFELY between my brother and me, with Pan and Vane in the lead. The night is cool and the wolves are howling.

The air feels wrong and I'm not sure what to make of it.

But the wolves are a good sign. Nani always said wolves were a symbol of protection and strength. They better be a good omen for what's to come. If we are to go against Tilly, Pan needs to claim his shadow and quickly.

Perhaps that's what feels wrong—clashing with our sister is like a garment that doesn't fit, that itches on our skin.

I don't want to hate my sister and yet the anger feels very close to hate.

She knew what our father intended to do and she was going to go along with it. Disinherit us, marry a pirate, overthrow Peter Pan.

Have Bash and I not done everything we were supposed to do to become kings? We took the endless hours of court decorum and etiquette lessons. We studied ancient texts to learn the ways of our ancestors. We practiced fae magic and spent hours in the yard going over sword techniques and fighting stances until our legs shook and our muscles ached.

And what did our dear sister do? She learned how to embroider tapestries and how to whittle court gossip into sharp weapons.

She used us, in a way, and I'm not sure I'll ever forgive her for it.

But the entire time we've been with Pan, there was always a little kernel of hope that she'd rescind our banishment and welcome us back into the fold, without condition or contract.

Now that hope is gone and the loss of it feels like the loss of a rib bone, like I can't find a comfortable way to stand.

Darling holds back a step and hooks her arm through mine. "I can feel you brooding."

"I'm not brooding," I say while I brood.

"What is it?"

I look ahead on the road as Hook's territory nears, which means if I took a left at any point in the road, I'd be headed toward fae territory. The pull on it is still very real and its nearness makes me ache.

Moonlight skims over Darling's face as she peers up at me from beneath the feathered fringe of her lashes. "I'm angry at my sister," I admit, "and I wish I wasn't."

Bash comes up on the other side of Darling and slings his arm around her shoulders. "He hates that we have to kill her."

"*Wait*...you do?"

Darling sounds just as sick about the prospect as I feel.

"She's not going to stop until we do," Bash adds. "I'm fine with it. I've said my peace to the universe."

"If only I could be so detached," I retort.

"It's either her or you, brother. You should always pick you."

I frown at him over the top of Darling's head. "She's our sister."

"And she betrayed us."

True enough. I just want to take Tilly by the arms and shake her until she turns back into our dear little sister who looked up at us like we were her heroes. Back then we were. We would have done anything for her. In fact, we did.

"What happens to the fae court if she's dead?" Darling asks.

Bash and I look at one another again.

What, indeed, Bash says. *Do we plan to return to the palace? Send Darling between our houses like a child of divorced parents?*

I turn back to the road and sense Pan's ear turned toward us. I don't think he can speak our language anymore, but sometimes I suspect he remembers a word or two.

I will do nothing to betray him. That, I am absolutely sure of.

We can figure it out if and when the time comes.

Of course it'll come. Just like us in the Darling's pussy.

I whack him upside the back of the head, which causes him to laugh at the sky.

"Quiet," Pan says as we finally cross into Hook's territory.

The air immediately changes once we're in pirate land. It's more chaotic but also somehow less wild than in Pan's territory.

Like a joker stuffed in a three-piece suit. It's as if the energy of Hook's land is an echo of the man himself. He's always been trying to be something he's not. Less pirate, more gentleman. I heard he was born in England to a noble family, but there's a reason he's here on Neverland with pirates for crew and not back in his home country living a respectable life.

The fact that he has yet to embrace that reality might be part of the reason he's such a world-class prick.

We keep walking, the gravel crunching beneath our boots. The closer we get, the more chaotic the night's energy, and the hair rises along my arms.

"You feel that?" I say to no one in particular.

Our pace has slowed.

"What is it?" Bash asks, searching the darkness.

"That's my shadow," Pan replies. "It's agitated."

"What does that mean?" Darling asks.

"It means someone has it cornered," Pan says.

33

PETER PAN

Since the moment my shadow crossed over to Hook's territory, I've not been particularly worried that Hook would take it. I've always regarded him as an annoying, ugly weed that sprung up on Neverland soil. A weed that no matter what I do, I cannot eradicate.

He is, or *was*, more nuisance than threat.

When he took Wendy from me, my opinion changed of him just *slightly*.

And then he traded Cherry for Smee and reinforced my opinion.

Who the fuck trades their own family as hostage?

There was always a little part of me that felt bad for Cherry. Forced into the position she was, tossed around and around like a skeleton leaf caught in a whirlpool with no hope of ever escaping the inescapable force working against her.

I'm not entirely sure trading her back is to her benefit.

Maybe neither situation is. She wants Vane and she won't have him now. Not since he's found a way to our Darling.

Darling is stuck with him. When Vane decides he'll have something, nothing will stop him from keeping it.

Now that we're all standing in the middle of the road that leads straight to Hook's house on the bay, I can't help but wonder if I should have worried about him more than I did. Or at the very least, if I should have made sure to bring Cherry with us.

She was an insurance policy, and one I've clearly overlooked in her usefulness.

Because I'm almost fucking certain Hook has hold of my shadow. I can feel it struggling, the energy of it vibrating. There's panic too...like it's...trapped, maybe?

I lock my hands behind my head and turn a circle in the road as the others stand by waiting for me to decide what the fuck we're going to do. If Hook has my shadow, then he knows without a doubt why I want into his territory and that I lied about my reasons in the first place. And if he has my shadow, he'll either use it against me or try to claim it for himself.

Does that pretentious asshole really think he can take *my* shadow? Everyone is always trying to take what is rightfully mine.

"Boys," I say and come to a stop in a slant of moonlight. "What do you say we kill some pirates?"

Vane cocks his head to the side. "Obviously, I will not turn down an opportunity to spill pirate blood."

Bash laughs. "Spill Hook's blood, he might faint at the sight of it."

"I got another idea." I look at Vane. "How fast can you fly back to the house?"

Vane retrieves the object stuffed in one of my dresser drawers and returns with it in less than fifteen minutes. By then we're halfway to the bay on Hook's end of the island.

"This the one?" Vane asks and holds up the object, the glass glinting in the moonlight.

"That's the one." I slip it into my pocket where it settles next to the lagoon seashell.

"Something else you should know," Vane adds. "On my way back, I saw a few pirates slinking up the beach toward the treehouse."

"Fuck." This is why we brought Darling with us. But I don't like taking her deep into pirate territory either. Like Cherry, there is no good option.

"Bash and Kas, when we get close to Hook's house, I want you to stay in the woods with our Darling. Vane and I will go into the house. If that's where he's keeping the shadow, I'll know once we're close."

The twins nod.

"Everyone know their place?" I ask.

They all nod their agreement, even Darling. I can't wait for this to be over so I can bury my cock inside of her, flush with power. She'll be trembling beneath me by sunrise.

There is a small town that sits on the hillside above the bay with Hook's house at the top of the hill so he can lord over his territory like a king.

The road forks—up the hill and to the left is Hook's house, to the right the road spills into town and the bay. Despite the late hour, the town glows brightly like a beacon against the night. Voices carry up the hill. I've always heard Hook's town is for men and women with little to no prospects and even less honor.

We go left to where my shadow is buzzing somewhere just out of my reach. We leave the road halfway up and slink through the night.

"Wait here," I tell the twins. "I'll whistle if we need you to move. Got it?"

They both nod and position Darling into a grove of birch trees. "Good luck," Kas says.

Before I leave, Darling wraps me in a hug. It catches me off-guard and I know she must feel the stiffness in my body. It takes me several long seconds to sink into her embrace.

"I'll be back," I tell her.

"I know." When she pulls away, she eyes Vane, but neither of them moves to touch.

"*We'll* be back," I correct and Darling nods before Vane and I turn away.

Hook is expecting me, so we return to the road when his house comes into view. If I didn't hate him so much, I might come to appreciate that he built his house to look like a big treehouse.

It stands on the hillside between three large oaks with several private and shared balconies that overlook the bay. It smells like cigars when we walk up the wide front steps and we find several pirates smoking and gathered around a wrought iron table.

"Should we start killing now?" Vane asks beneath his breath.

"Best save our shot for when we really need it."

The pirates eye us steadily like they know something we don't.

The unease sinks like a weight in my gut.

Vane stays in step with me as we enter the house of my enemy. It makes my skin crawl. It makes me want to start tipping over vases and smashing lamps on the floor. I've forgotten how my war with Hook began, but I'm not sure it matters anymore because the hate is so vivid, somedays it feels like a living, breathing thing.

I very much detest the man and everything he stands for.

"Which way?" Vane says, keeping his voice low.

I try to shake the feeling that we're walking into a trap and go to the left.

My shadow is so close now, I can feel its power disrupting the air like an electrical storm.

"What are the chances we get in and out with no one noticing us?" Vane asks.

"I suspect—"

"Peter Pan."

My hair bristles. My teeth grit.

The sound of Hook's voice is like sandpaper dragging over my knuckles. Every muscle in my body tenses up.

"I assure you, your *lost* Lost Boy isn't here in my house." Hook comes down the grand staircase, his hands clasped behind his back. He's wearing one of those ridiculous over-coats with gold embroidery around the collar and down the lapel. He's ditched the stupid fucking tights and buckled shoes and has replaced both with more practical trousers and leather boots.

"I think we both know I'm not looking for a Lost Boy," I say.

Hook smiles at me, all bright white teeth. "Whatever do you mean?"

There's this energy to Hook that is part ego, part obliviousness. He thinks he's better than me, but he's just a man with so many weaknesses, I'd have to sit down to list them all.

He is not better than me.

He might be more ambitious, however.

I glance around the house. "Where is it?" From this vantage point, I can only see the foyer, half of a sitting room and a large hall to my left that leads to what looks like a library. If I've been inside this house, I don't remember it.

"Where is what?" Hook stops on the bottom step and unclasps his hands, letting his hook come forward. The metal gleams in the light. It's hard not to look at it when I'm the one who helped cause the need for it.

That, I do remember. I remember the way Hook screamed at the sight of his own blood. How the Crocodile dragged his finger through the crimson and then ran his tongue over the length of his finger, cleaning off the blood.

I remember how Hook fainted after that and the Crocodile laughed like it was all one big joke.

That fucker is scarier than Vane.

I both admire him and fear him.

Hook fears him more than me, though, and I intend to use it against him.

"I'm going to ask you one more time, James. Where's my fucking shadow?"

Hook's jaw flexes as he looks at me down the aristocratic slope of his nose. "I already told you, I don't know. Besides, aren't you missing one from your party? Where's Cherry?"

His voice cracks on her name and he flinches at the sound, blinking away the emotion that creeps into his face.

My shadow grows more frenzied. It's definitely contained, wherever it is. I know it's nearby. But not near enough.

I surge to the left toward the library when a gun goes off.

The wood trim around the open double doors explodes as the musket ball shreds it.

I come to a stop.

"I wouldn't go any further if I were you," Hook warns.

I slowly turn around to find Smee behind Vane, a gun pointed at the back of his head. His teeth are gritted but his violet eye has turned black. There are more pirates behind Smee, hands on their pistols.

Vane and I could take Hook and Smee no problem. We might even be able to handle the additional pirates.

I meet Vane's gaze and try to gauge his interest in letting go of the shadow so it can do its fucking thing.

He's practically vibrating from the effort of holding it at bay.

I give him a barely noticeable nod of my head, but just as the Dark Shadow comes out to play, the fae queen slams through the door, our Darling caught in her grasp.

34

PETER PAN

THE TWINS LOOK LIKE THEY'RE HIGH, EYES GLASSY AND
unfocused. It takes me a second to realize they're trapped in
an illusion.

Darling is coherent though, with Tilly's long nails
threaded through her hair, her hand splayed over the top of
Darling's head.

I hold up my hands. "All right. You've got me. Now what
do you plan to do with me?"

I don't really care. I'm just trying to stall them.

Tilly laughs. "What do we plan to do? We want you
dead. So consider this the invitation to your funeral."

"Wait," Hook says, teeth gritted. "I need to know how to
claim the shadow before you off him."

"Don't worry, Hook. I'm sure we can figure it out."

"Tilly, you always were too proud for your own good,"
I say.

There are several fae with her, all of them dressed in the
court's dark battle gear, the cloth embroidered in iridescent

thread, the shoulders and elbows outfitted with reticulated leather plates.

"Quite the outfits you all have there," I say. "Tell me, do you polish your shiny leather boots before every battle too?"

Tilly's mouth thins just as the room sways around me.

"I know what you're doing," I bite out as the darkness floats in and the air takes on the scent of wet earth. "Your illusions won't work on me."

Tilly fights me and my mind for another half minute before giving up with a huff. "Very well. Kill him."

"Wait!" Hook steps between us. "My sister. They didn't bring her."

"Is that what you're concerned about? You do realize these are my brothers. I'm literally risking their lives for this coup. And you're worried about your sister, who's been living with them for years?"

Hook's nostrils flare as he inhales and schools his features. "I would just like some kind of proof that she's okay or near. What if they did something to her? Or hid her? How would I ever find her?"

"Did you?" Tilly asks me. "Did you do something to Cherry?"

Certainly worth the bluff.

"I guess you'll find out once I'm dead, won't you?"

Tilly's grip shifts on Darling and Darling cries out from a fresh wave of pain, the ache of it etching in the fine lines around her eyes.

My heart drops. "Stop!" I surge forward and the pirates lift their guns. The fae arm their bows.

I freeze.

Tilly wrenches Darling back. "Answer the question so we can get on with this."

I meet Hook's gaze. I don't want to see any kind of emotion on his face. He didn't seem to have any care for Cherry when he traded her for Smee.

But that was then. And this is now.

And he's terrified we've done something to her. Maybe deep down he always knew he could get her back if she was at our house. Now he has no idea what to believe and no way of knowing the truth.

Now I'm glad we left her behind.

"Please," Hook says.

I do not like being coerced by something so human as empathy.

The desperation on Hook's face almost makes me change my mind.

Almost.

"She's in a metal box at the bottom of the ocean."

"No!" Hook screams right before he charges me.

35

PETER PAN

It's the distraction we need.

As Hook comes at me, Vane flies toward Darling and Tilly. The Dark One has always been fast, but he's faster when the Darling is in danger.

He has her scooped up in his arms before Tilly even realizes what's happening.

Good.

Hook barrels into me and I let him cart me backward right through the open library doors.

My shadow senses me and trembles, wherever it is.

There's shouting in the next room and several guns go off.

Right before Hook slams me into a couch, I spot the twins on their feet, decimating the fae warriors with nothing but their fists.

Hook and I go down and then he rises above me, eyes wide, mouth cut into a slash as the anger takes over.

I have a temper, but Hook's is legendary.

His hand comes to my throat while his hook lashes out, catching me across the face. Blood immediately wells in the cut. He squeezes harder and a puff of air escapes me and lifts the sweat-soaked hair around his face.

"How could you!" he shouts.

"She...kicked...and...screamed the whole...way." He doesn't like that. He jabs his hook into my side and the tine pierces flesh. White hot pain lances through me.

But I'm more focused than ever and Hook is losing his fucking shit.

I reach into my pants pocket and pull out a watch.

The end of Hook's hook punctures deeper and the sharp pain sinks to bone, forcing tears to well in my eyes.

Working blindly, I feel out for the pin on the side of the watch and press it in.

Tick-tock.

Hook flinches.

Tick-tock-tick-tock.

Terror ebbs into his face.

"No," he says on a choked breath. "*He's here.*"

Tick-tock-tick...

He stumbles away and clutches his hook to his chest. "No, no, no."

As blood runs down my side drenching my shirt, I struggle to my feet and scan the room. My shadow is somewhere here. I can feel it.

Hook backpedals into the corner and sinks to the floor, his arms shielding his head. It's so fucking easy to get to him.

In the other room, Kas is beating one of the pirates with a marble bust. Blood is painting the air. Tilly is circling Bash, her wings bright crimson and fluttering behind her.

Vane and the Darling are nowhere in sight.

There are cabinets at the bottom of every section of bookcases and I start opening doors, looking inside. I find a rectangular chest in the third one. The chest rocks when I crouch down beside it.

"There you are, you little fucker."

The chest rattles again.

I grab one of the leather straps and yank it out, then retrieve the seashell just to be on the safe side.

"Here it fucking goes. Don't you dare run away from me again."

I flip the latch.

36

WINNIE

I'm flying. And clutched in Vane's arms, held tightly against the solid line of his body.

"Don't look down, Darling," he says, his voice rising to cut in across the wind.

I don't know how fast we're going but it feels faster than a jet plane.

I have no choice but to cling to him and keep my eyes slammed shut. I'm not quite ready for this level of magic—to be flying among the clouds with nothing beneath me.

Maybe someday I will be but not today.

Vane puts us down just outside of the cold bonfire. The house is quiet in front of us, but there are shadows sliding past the windows.

"Pirates," Vane says on a growl.

"What do we do?"

"*We* do nothing. *I* fucking kill them." He takes my hand in his and slinks through the back yard, then up the stairs and across the balcony. He moves silently, confidently, as if he's used to moving through the shadows, plotting murder as he goes.

Slowly, he opens the balcony door and then slips us inside.

We come up on the first pirate in the dining room and Vane puts his hands on the man's arms and lets his darkness seep into skin. The man convulses in Vane's grip and a strangled cry erupts from his throat.

His buddy hears it and comes running at me.

I yelp and dart away as his meaty hand snatches for me.

"Darling!" Vane yells and drops the man in his grip.

I slam into the kitchen island as the pirate advances. He's missing a front tooth and his hair is straggly and greasy, and he smells like he hasn't showered in a month.

"Come here!" He leers at me, swipes again, and I duck away, scooting around the island, and snatch one of the knives from the block on the counter.

He rounds on me and I don't think. I just stab upward.

It isn't until something wet and hot and sticky covers my arm that I know I've hit something vital. The man's eyes get wide as his head ticks and blood leaks out of his mouth with a meager cough.

"Get the fuck off me," I say and shove him.

He goes down in a sloppy mess just as Vane reaches us.

He looks at the man and then at me, the knife still clutched in my hand. "Well done, Darling."

God, I must be corrupt because hearing his praise after a murder makes me glow.

"Watch out!" Another pirate appears behind Vane. I throw him the knife and he plucks it from the air with no effort at all. He fists it in his hand and turns and stabs down like an ice pick. Once, twice, three times. So many times I stop counting. *Boom boom boom.*

Blood splatters and springs like a geyser and the man drops where he stands.

Vane turns to me covered in blood.

Fuck. Fuck, he is glorious.

"Are you all right?" he asks me.

"I'm fine."

He comes over to me and holds up my arms, checks my torso, then my neck.

"I said I'm okay."

The line of his jaw hardens. "You almost weren't."

"You have to get back," I say.

His teeth grit at the reminder.

"Go. Pan needs you."

"Get in his tomb. Lock the door behind you. Promise me." There are hard lines between his dark brows.

"I promise."

He nods and then turns away. And then—

He races back to me, grabs me by the jaw, and kisses me roughly. A contented sigh escapes him and then he's kissing me again and we slam against the nearest wall.

I am fucked up. That's official. Because I'm covered in blood and Vane is covered in blood and there are dead pirates littering the floor, but all I can think about is Vane's hands on my body. I'm wound up tight, heart pounding.

But no.

No.

I shove him back and he growls at me.

"Get the fuck out of here and go help Pan."

His mouth ticks. "Down to the tomb. Now."

"I'm going."

He darts out the door and immediately takes to the air.

And because I don't take my promises lightly, I make my way through the loft and past the Never Tree and—

"Winnie."

Cherry's meager voice catches me off guard and my heart leaps to my throat. "Shit. Cherry. You scared me."

"Sorry."

"What are you doing here? Are you okay?"

She licks her lips. "So, you and Vane?"

Oh shit. "Umm..."

"It's okay. I knew it would never last with him. I mean, I tried for a really long time. And then you came along. Of course he was going to pick you over me."

"Cherry, I'm—"

"It's okay."

But she doesn't look like it's okay.

"I really am sorry."

"I know." She blinks and drags a knuckle beneath her eye, mopping up a tear. "Can you help me with something? I heard a noise in my room."

"Oh no. It might be another pirate. We should go to—"

"No, I only saw the three," Cherry says. "I think it's one of the parakeets. I think it's trapped in my room. Can you help me get it out?"

I look between her and the hall to Pan's tomb. This will just take a second, right? And I feel so bad for Cherry. If she's asking for my help, I feel like it's the least I can do.

"All right. Real quick and then we have to get down to Pan's tomb."

"Of course," she says and follows me down the stairs to her room. "It'll just be real quick."

37

PETER PAN

TILLY SLAMS INTO ME FROM BEHIND AND THE CHEST'S LID FLIES
open and my shadow darts out.

Motherfucking fuck.

The fae queen shoves her blade into my gut and I exhale
in a rush.

"Your time is up, Never King," she says through gritted
teeth. She's easily a foot shorter than I am, but I've under-
estimated the strength of the fae queen.

The blade hits bone and my vision goes white.

"Bash!" I yell. "Kas!"

Tilly's eyes narrow and the room slips away. I'm back at
the lagoon, but the water is dark and the trees are dead.

"No," I say to Tilly and swim my way back to reality.

She plants her hand on my forehead and shoves me
back in.

The sky grows dark and the wind picks up.

This is the Neverland that terrifies me. The one that has
no shadow and no king.

I wrap my hand around Tilly's wrist and the connection brings me back, blink by blink.

"You betrayed me," I tell Tilly. "Just like your fucking mother."

She screams at me, driving the blade deeper, and I cough up blood.

"Give me the shell!" Vane yells and I'm so relieved to see him, I almost weep.

I fetch it from my pocket and toss it to him.

He holds it up and my shadow grows still in the far corner of the library.

Tilly pulls her knife from my gut and races toward Vane just as her brothers run into the room and tackle her.

My shadow leaps from the corner and disappears into the shell.

Vane turns to me, tossing the shell back.

When I snatch it from the air, my arm vibrates with the connection of energy.

I drop the shell to the floor, smash it with my boot, and hunch to all fours over it.

And my shadow finally comes home.

38

BASH

OUR DEAR SISTER TAKES ONE LOOK AT PAN CLAIMING HIS SHADOW and leaps out the nearest window.

Never thought I'd see the fae queen running with her tail tucked between her legs, but goddamn, do I enjoy seeing our sister bested.

I'm covered in pirate and fae blood, and the fae blood glitters in just the right slant of light.

I'm not sure how I feel about fighting my own people, but I guess I have to get right with it real quick if I'm to overthrow my sister.

Pan's still on all fours breathing heavily, back arched.

The air vibrates around him.

I don't remember what he was like with his shadow. That was long before my time.

But I'm not surprised that the difference between Pan with his shadow and Pan without is the difference between a sunny day and a raging storm.

It's an energy that rolls up my arms and down my spine.

I suddenly have the urge to get to my knees.

It reminds me of the same feeling I had when our father donned his formal court uniform on a fae solstice.

Something bigger than myself. Something unspeakably magical.

When Pan gets to his feet and slowly rises to a stand, I gulp down air.

Fuuuuuuck.

He looks the same and he is the same height and he takes up the same space, but somehow, he has grown in size.

Goosebumps trail up my arms. The hair lifts on the back of my neck.

I know now that I picked the right side.

Pan is fucking scary as fuck on a good day. With his shadow?

There have always been whispers on the island that he is a god. No one knows where he came from, including him.

Now I think I believe the rumors.

Now I think they might be true.

Before I know what I'm doing, I'm kneeling on the floor. And my brother kneels beside me, and behind us Hook still cowers in a ball.

"What the fuck are we doing?" Kas whispers.

"Fuck if I know."

"If you think I'm bowing to you," Vane says, "you've got another thing coming."

"Get up," Pan tells us.

Kas and I rise and Pan comes over. I try not to shrink again like a trembling dipshit. I'm a king in my own right. The fuck do I have to be submissive about?

I have to recalibrate what I think and know about Pan now that he's got his shadow back.

"Thank you," Pan says and I swear his blue eyes glow a little more.

"We made our choice," Kas says and I nod in agreement.

Pan grips us both by the shoulder and gives us a squeeze. And then he goes over to Hook, grabs him by the throat and wrenches him to his feet.

"Bloody hell," Hook says on a grunt.

"You are a man who can make his own choices," Pan says. "But if you choose to stand against me, you're making the wrong one."

Hook's face turns red as he struggles for air. "Help me... stand against...the Crocodile and we...have a deal."

"This isn't a negotiation," Pan says.

"Worth...a...shot."

Pan looks at Vane over his shoulder and Vane shrugs.

"I'll think about it." Pan drops Hook to the floor and he lands like a bag of bones.

Hook coughs and sputters. "What about Cherry?"

I snort. "She's been at the house the entire time. I take it you're not very good at playing poker?"

"You bastards—"

"Just be glad she's alive," Pan says as he makes his way for the door. "Come," he says to us. "I have a Darling I need to get home to."

"We all do," I remind him.

He meets my gaze and I have to suppress a shiver. "Yes," he answers. "Let's all go home to our Darling."

39

CHERRY

My hands are so clammy, I have to keep wiping them on my pants as Winnie makes her way downstairs.

What am I doing?

Maybe I should stop her. She did apologize.

But I keep seeing her with Vane in the woods and it makes me want to scream and cry and vomit.

It hurts so bad, it feels like I could die from it.

Better Winnie than me. It wasn't so bad before she came. The twins would sometimes share me and every now and then, I'd catch Vane regarding me like he might devour me.

I want that back.

Winnie changed everything.

We go down the hallway to my closed bedroom door.

"Here," I say and my voice wobbles. "Let me."

Winnie frowns at me but steps aside.

I can't breathe.

I turn the knob and crack the door open.

Winnie steps over the threshold.

I shove her all the way in.

"*Hey*. Cherry!"

I slam the door closed behind her and grab the door knob and lean back with all of my weight.

"Cherry!" she yells and wrenches on the knob. I grit my teeth. Slam my eyes closed. I can't do this. I *can* do this. I have to do this. Who cares about a Darling? There've been so many. They'll forget about her eventually, just like they've forgotten about all the others.

"Cherry!"

Her voice is rising in panic. Something growls.

"Oh my god. Cherry. Open the door."

She screams. Something thuds against the wall.

I keep hanging on. Hang on. Just a little longer.

"Cherry, please!"

There's a loud snarl. The sound of glass breaking.

Tears well in my eyes as my heart races in the space between my ears.

And then...

Silence.

I keep holding onto the door.

I'm terrified of opening it.

Will the shadow just race out past me? Do I have to worry about it? Will there be blood? What will I find left of Winnie?

Maybe if I duck out of the way...

Light spills from the crack beneath the door.

A shadow stretches in it.

What the—

I straighten, wipe my hands again on my pants, and then reach out for the doorknob, hands shaking the entire time.

My shirt is thumping on my chest, my heart is racing so fast.

I turn the knob and push the door in.

It creaks on its hinges and I spot Winnie in the middle of my room, standing among the wreckage of all of my favorite things.

Her back is to me.

"Winnie?"

She says nothing.

I lick my lips and inhale deeply.

"Winnie?"

She slowly turns to me.

I'm practically vibrating.

And when she finally faces me and lifts her chin—

Her eyes are darkest black.

If you'd like to continue on the adventure with Winnie and her Lost Boys, be sure to pre-order book three so you don't miss out!

Pre-order Their Vicious Darling now!

And if you want to get sneak peeks at Their Vicious Darling as its written and get early access to book news and cover reveals, be sure to sign-up for Nikki's Newsletter.
https://www.subscribepage.com/nikkistcrowe

ALSO BY NIKKI ST. CROWE

ABOUT THE AUTHOR

Nikki St. Crowe has been writing for as long as she can remember. Her first book, written in the 4th grade, was about a magical mansion full of treasure. While she still loves writing about magic, she's ditched the treasure for something better: villains, monsters, and anti-heroes, and the women who make them wild.

These days, when Nikki isn't writing or daydreaming about villains, she can either be found on the beach or at home with her husband and daughter.

Nikki's Newsletter
https://www.subscribepage.com/nikkistcrowe

Follow Nikki on TikTok
https://www.tiktok.com/@nikkistcrowe

Gain early access to cover reveals and sneak peeks on Patreon:
https://www.patreon.com/nikkistcrowe

Join Nikki's Reader Group:
https://www.facebook.com/groups/nikkistcrowesnest/

Visit Nikki on the web at:
www.nikkistcrowe.com

tiktok.com/@nikkistcrowe

instagram.com/nikkistcrowe

amazon.com/Nikki-St-Crowe/e/B098PJW25Y

bookbub.com/profile/nikki-st-crowe